PUFFIN BOOKS
Editor: Kaye Webb
PS271

SPEED SIX!

The three owners of the Eds and Vins garage
for old cars were full of gloom as they faced
the certainty that they would have to close
down for lack of sales. It was a brainwave
touched with madness to put their adored
Speed Six Bentley *Diane* through the gruelling
twenty-four-hour test of speed and endurance
at Le Mans, competing against cars a generation younger and a generation more
advanced.

Excitement soon reached boiling point,
when they realized that their close neighbours and rivals would stick at nothing in
order to win. Time for preparation was short,
and sabotage had never entered their heads,
nor the idea that their opponents might
deliberately force them off the track in the
race. Dangerous anyway, this Le Mans was
more dangerous than ever, and grew more
desperately exciting as one by one competitors dropped out, and *Diane* at last came
within reach of glory.

For boys of twelve and over.

*Cover photograph by Montagu Motor
Museum, Beaulieu*

D1437708

BRUCE CARTER

Speed Six!

PENGUIN BOOKS

Penguin Books Ltd, Harmondsworth, Middlesex, England
Penguin Books Pty Ltd, Ringwood, Victoria, Australia
—
First published by The Bodley Head 1953
Rewritten specially for this edition and published in Puffin Books 1966
—
Copyright © Bruce Carter, 1953, 1966
—
Made and printed in Great Britain
by Cox & Wyman Ltd, London, Reading and Fakenham

Set in Monotype Baskerville

Contents

AUTHOR'S NOTE

This is a story about a real motor race, the great Le Mans twenty-four-hour event for sports cars, and about a real motor car, the great Speed Six vintage Bentley.

After their successive victories from 1927 to 1930, I always longed for someone to enter a real Bentley at Le Mans again. If you take into account that the road was rougher, narrower, and with sharper corners when the Speed Six last won, then until the 1950s (when I imagine this story to have happened) it was not absolutely impossible, the rules permitting, that a Speed Six could again have kept up with the fastest cars.

So if this story is imagined for enjoyment, let us not forget that it could, perhaps have happened.

February 1966   *Bruce Carter*

Chapter 1

A Bentley at Le Mans?

'AND what on earth,' asked Johnny Wild in amazement, 'is that supposed to mean?'

Danny Black gave a final touch to the last 'S' and looked down at his friend with a resigned expression. 'It's high time those things you are pleased to call brain cells grew up,' he said with a sigh. '"Eds and Vins" – "Edwardian and Vintage,"' he explained. 'And if any customer asks, do try to remember that Edwardian cars are those built between 1905 and 1916, and Vintage cars between 1919 and 1930.'

Johnny nodded obediently. '"And we do not deal in jelly-bodied tinware."' He quoted the catch-phrase that had given their garage its high reputation among the connoisseurs of classic cars. '"Eds and Vins." So that's what we're going to call ourselves now. Not bad, Blackie.'

Blackie climbed down from his ladder and looked up at the new sign critically. 'Well, it may make them curious enough to stop and ask what it's all about,' he said. 'And that's half the battle. The other half's yours, Johnny.'

Ever since they had established their garage four years before, it had fallen on Johnny to be the salesman. Too un-mechanical to handle the technical work, too careless and light-hearted for book-keeping, finance, and general organization, salesmanship was the only thing left for Johnny. And the reason why they had survived for as long as they had, with their stubborn refusal to

handle any car built after 1930, was Johnny's tremendous sales ability.

The steadier, better-balanced Danny Black – a keen
slogger with a good head for figures – they had mutually
agreed should be general manager; while the third
member of the trio, the Welshman, Mervyn Williams,
who had been engineering officer in Johnny and
Blackie's squadron during the war, was head mechanic.

So, with their new signboard still wet and gleaming in
the early-morning sun, it was now to be: 'Eds and Vins,
Ltd; Danny Black, Accountant and General Manager;
Jonathan Wild, Chief Sales Executive and Test Driver;
Mervyn Williams, Superintendent Engineering Depart-
ment.'

It sounded wonderful. They had a good stock of cars –
thirty-seven examples of automobile engineering at its
finest, from a gleaming 1925 Rolls-Royce 20 h.p. to a
vast 1928 Belgian Minerva. They had all the enthusiasm
in the world. All they lacked was money.

For 'Eds and Vins, Ltd' was dead, flat, hopelessly
broke.

'Tea up,' came a loud voice from the main workshop.
Mervyn Williams had the morning brew ready.

They might be on the verge of bankruptcy, but there
was always tea. Tea – hot, strong, sweet tea in huge
chipped mugs – flowed freely at 'Eds and Vins'. It was
nearly as potent as the fuel Johnny insisted they should
use for testing their higher-performance vehicles.

Johnny and Blackie strolled in together towards the
sound of the welcome voice. 'I don't know that a new
name and a shiny new sign's going to bring the customers flocking in,' said Blackie gloomily, 'but we've got to
do something to stop the rot.'

'Is it as grim as all that?' asked Johnny.

8

'Three pounds, seventeen shillings in the bank,' Blackie told him.

'Phew! That calls for a drink,' Johnny exclaimed, reaching down for one of the steaming mugs balanced on a petrol can. 'I'd no idea things were as bad as that. Hey, Mervyn,' he called to the little Welshman emerging from the dark, noisy interior of the workshop, 'did you know we were flatters?'

Blackie glanced with amusement at Johnny's lean, bony face, which showed no trace of worried concern for their future. Johnny had never really worried in all his life, even with five Messerschmitts on his tail on a fighter sweep. In a few minutes he would have forgotten entirely about their money troubles.

Mervyn Williams may have been a famed engineer, but he was not famous for raising depressed spirits. Mervyn the Glum he had been called in his time, and Johnny's announcement served only to deepen the lines of hopeless despair that spanned his heavy brow.

He grunted and buried his face in his tea mug. 'Everything turns out for the worst,' he muttered, which was one of his favourite cheerful sayings.

'Except *Diane*,' Johnny reminded him.

'Humph – yes, except *Diane*,' Mervyn had to admit.

The three of them glanced lovingly at the massive dark green Bentley standing in front of all their other cars like a glittering sentinel. This wonderful old Speed Six was not only the best preserved and fastest vintage Bentley in the world. It was believed to be the only survivor of the Speed Six Bentley team which had triumphed at Le Mans in 1930 – and their own *Diane* had been the winner. Even Mervyn, who had used all his engineering genius to bring it to a state of mechanical perfection, had been known to gaze at *Diane* with tears in his eyes.

9

Blackie had spent hours on the paintwork, had re-trimmed the seats in best-quality hide, and had brought the dashboard back to its original state. Finally, Johnny had tested the Speed Six up and down the runways of the old disused airfield behind their garage, reporting to Mervyn the results of the high-speed tuning he had been carrying out on the engine.

All three were wondering who would have the courage to speak the fateful but inevitable words. They came at last after a long silence from Blackie – Danny Black the businessman: '*Diane* will have to go,' he said quietly, as though presiding at a funeral service.

The other two nodded agreement. 'I'm afraid you're right,' Johnny said. 'There's nothing else for it. There may be a slump in vintage-car demand, but a Speed Six Bentley' – and he shrugged his sturdy shoulders – 'well, there'd be a hundred enthusiasts here within an hour, bidding each other up madly.'

Blackie strolled over to the car, still holding his steaming mug of tea. He put one arm lovingly over the leather-strapped bonnet and murmured, '*Diane*, old girl, you're going to have to go,' just as if he were talking to a very old dog for whom the vet had been called in.

Without further word, Johnny climbed into the driver's seat and Mervyn Williams raised one side of the hinged bonnet and gazed reverently at the engine – a vast masterpiece of mechanics, resplendent with polished copper tubing and gleaming S.U. carburettors.

Blackie raised his mug. 'I propose a toast to *Diane*, the greatest Bentley of them all,' he said.

They all took a sip of tea. 'And may her new owner appreciate her quality and attend her needs as if she were a goddess.'

'As indeed she is,' murmured Mervyn.

Johnny adjusted the ignition and hand-throttle settings and called out, 'Stand clear, I'm starting her up.'

Mervyn clipped and screwed back the bonnet, and they both stepped back as Johnny pressed the starter. The great $6\frac{1}{2}$-litre engine at once roared into life, its healthy exhaust note crackling across the silent runways of the airfield beyond.

Blackie listened with awed respect, thinking to himself that no sports car engine today could give such an impression of massive power and reliability. 'They just don't make them like that now,' he said to Mervyn standing beside him, and the Welshman nodded dourly in agreement.

Johnny raised his hand from the wheel and shouted across, 'Throw over my gloves and goggles; I'm going to give her a last run.'

Johnny kept them handy in the office, ready for the race meetings in which he took part almost every week-end. As Blackie handed them to him, Johnny said, 'Come on, we may as well preside over these last rites together. I'll show you what *Diane* can do, in spite of her old age.'

Mervyn Williams glowered while Blackie clambered into the passenger seat. 'You take her gently, man,' he warned. 'A fine thing it'll be if you break up our last asset.'

Johnny grinned and gave the thumbs-up sign. 'I promise not to break the sound barrier,' he shouted out with a laugh. 'You know me, Mervyn, safe and steady as a boy on his first scooter.'

Mervyn snorted, and his face fell into its customary folds of gloom and despair. Johnny revved up the Bentley and engaged first gear. 'Come and join us for a spin,' he called to their chief mechanic. 'Plenty of room for a third.' There was a mischievous grin on his face as he beckoned Mervyn invitingly, for Johnny and Blackie had known for years that Mervyn was suspicious of anything that moved on four wheels, and that he was nothing less than terrified of the Speed Six. Mervyn Williams could spend happy days and weeks bringing an old engine to a state of perfection, but the moment power was transmitted to the wheels, he preferred to leave motor-cars severely alone. 'I'll get the last bit of h.p. out of any old heap you put in my workshop – I'll even manage your racing from the pits,' he had once confided to the other two, 'but you may as well know that I don't hold with speed. Ten m.p.h. on my bike's good enough for me.'

Mervyn grunted in disgust and turned away at the invitation. Up on the bench he had a Lagonda engine which he had rebored, and he was in the middle of grinding in the valves. That was precision work requiring real skill. Racing *Diane* round the airfield with that maniac Johnny indeed! He hunched up his shoulders and disappeared into the familiar welcoming gloom of his workshop, with its pleasant smell of oil.

'There's never been a car like this, Blackie my boy,' shouted Johnny. 'Positive steering that holds a perfect line around corners – sticks to the road like a leech – perfectly spaced gear ratios – faultless brakes. This is motoring, real motoring.'

Johnny was in a trance of delight. There was no other car in which everything was so 'just right'; and no car of its age that could approach it for sheer performance.

'Ah, bliss – what bliss!' he murmured. He pointed at the speedometer needle. 'Now watch this,' he told Blackie.

He swung *Diane* off the narrow perimeter track of the airfield and on to one of the mile-and-a-half long runways. From where he sat, Johnny could see the long, dark green bonnet ending in a brief flash of the shining radiator. Beyond were the two front wheels beneath the graceful Vanden Plas mudguards, the straight length of unbroken macadam stretching into the distance.

'Just clear the plugs.' And he raced the engine several times in case they had oiled up during the idling. Then he released the outside handbrake, eased himself more comfortably into the bucket seat, and pulled his goggles down over his eyes.

The two tons of steel moved forward. Johnny gave a touch of pressure to the throttle, and *Diane* gathered speed, at first slowly, and then with a sound like thunder rolling across a plain as Johnny put his foot hard down.

Up to 30 m.p.h. in first, 55 m.p.h. in second, the rev. counter needle swinging back at each change, only to climb steadily across the dial to the 3,000 r.p.m. mark. At 78 m.p.h. Johnny pulled the stubby gear lever back into top and settled down to fast driving in earnest.

Blackie glanced across at Johnny, who always sat bolt upright at the wheel, his shoulders against the back of the seat, relaxed and at ease as every good racing driver should be. His arms were almost fully stretched out to the big metal steering wheel, his eyes – except for sudden darting looks down at the instrument panel – remained fixed intently on the road ahead. 'Oh, but he's enjoying himself,' Blackie thought with amusement. 'This is our Johnny at his best – and there's no one to touch him when he gets behind the wheel.' And he remembered all the tempting offers manufacturers' team managers had made him to drive their cars for a season's racing – all of which Johnny had turned down. 'Pouf, I wouldn't touch their filthy new tinware with disinfected rubber gloves,' Johnny had exploded when the last offer had arrived in the post. But Blackie knew Johnny would give his right arm to get into big-time racing if his loyalty to their garage and to vintage cars was not so strong.

Johnny's lean face broke into a grin. 'Watch this for steadiness,' he shouted against the roar of the wind.

He began to swing the car from side to side, turning the wheel to and fro violently. Blackie clutched the door-sill to prevent himself from being flung out of the Bentley. But the chassis hardly rocked an inch and there was no sound of protest from the tyres. This was where the hard springing and the superb suspension system paid dividends; and all the time the car was being thrown first one way and then the other, the speedometer needle remained firmly on 110 m.p.h.

'Ah!' sighed Johnny under his breath, 'what a motor-car!'

The trees bordering the end of the runway were looming up at an alarming rate. Johnny eased off speed and dabbed the brake pedal once or twice. Then he double-declutched with a great roar of revs, and flicked the gear lever into third, following this movement with a touch back on the outside brake handle.

There was still sixty-five on the speedometer when he pulled the car to the right of the runway and set her into a drift on to the narrow perimeter track that encircled the airfield.

Diane came to a halt as smoothly and steadily as a school bus half a mile along the rough track, its slow, regular tick-over exhaust note echoing back from the pinewoods alongside.

'That was some going,' commented Blackie. No mean driver himself, he appreciated only too well both *Diane*'s astonishing performance and Johnny's wonderful handling of the big machine.

Johnny brushed back his long black hair and pushed his goggles on to his forehead. 'Blackie lad,' he sighed, 'it's a cruel fate having to sell this beauty. We'll never see another like *Diane*.' He suddenly looked sharply ahead, and pulled himself up by the windscreen. 'Take a look at this, Blackie,' he said, pointing to a low silver dot fast approaching them down the track. 'Well, I'll be . . .'

'It's one of the Atlantics,' Blackie confirmed excitedly. 'And it's moving, too.'

The Atlantic Competition Unit, a branch of the massive Coventry combine of Atlantic Motors, Ltd, manufacturers of cheap, mass-produced family cars, and much more expensive, high-performance sports cars, was based on the other side of the disused airfield from 'Eds and Vins'. The tuning, testing, and preparation of Atlantics for the important sports car events of the racing season took place, under the direction of an unsavoury and domineering body named Barnaby James, in a group of rebuilt R.A.F. huts similar to those used by Johnny, Blackie, and Mervyn Williams.

From time to time Barnaby James used the airfield runways for high-speed experimental work. One of Atlantic's low, streamlined little cars was darting towards Johnny and Blackie now, the roar of its healthy open exhaust sounding above the tick-over of *Diane*.

Johnny gave a short laugh of delight. 'Let's have a little dice,' he said, with a gleam of mischief in his eye. 'This could be fun.'

'All right,' Blackie agreed, dropping back into his seat. 'But take it easy, Johnny. If you smash up *Diane* we're really in the soup.'

The little two-seater shot past, heading for the runway. A goggled and helmeted figure behind the wheel

15

ignored them entirely. 'Uncivil little stuck-up . . .' muttered Johnny, but he was too busy turning the Bentley around to say more.

The low-slung Atlantic, its raw aluminium panels glinting in the sun, was already some way down the runway when Johnny pulled *Diane* around from the perimeter track in pursuit.

'Come on, *Diane*,' said Johnny aloud, 'show that little jazzed-up box of tricks what real motoring is.'

The Bentley shot forward, revelling in the fast revs, and Johnny and Blackie felt the back of the seats pressing hard and satisfyingly into their spines.

There was no doubt that the Atlantic driver was trying, especially after he caught a glimpse of the Bentley in his rear mirror. But it was more than he could do to throw the other car off his tail.

Johnny had his foot flat on the floor, and the gap narrowed as the two cars, one low, lean, and wicked-looking, the other tall, square, and as dignified and purposeful as a stage-coach, tore along that short straight flat out.

'You're holding him,' yelled Blackie excitedly. 'By golly, you're holding him!' Incredible though it seemed, the old car was doing better than that; slowly, at first hardly perceptibly, but then with growing speed, the gap between the two cars was narrowing, until the nose of the Bentley was running almost level with the low tail of the silver Atlantic.

It was not until he saw the red brake lights flickering on the little car that Blackie realized how near the end of the runway they were. There was barely a quarter of a mile to go, and Johnny still had his foot hard on the floor. Blackie glanced anxiously across at Johnny as he saw the grass edge and the deep ditch beyond tearing towards them. It was as if Johnny had forgotten how short the runway was in the excitement of the pursuit.

A crash seemed inevitable when Johnny at last switched his foot from the accelerator pedal to the brake. His right hand flashed to the outside lever, and then with an ear-splitting shriek of revs that sent the tachometer needle whipping round its dial, he threw the lever into third.

'You'll never do it,' called out Blackie, but his voice was lost in the shriek of the tyres and the screaming protest of the straining engine struggling to hold back the heavy mass of steel from destruction.

This was the sort of challenge Johnny loved. He had cut things fine, but he knew *Diane's* capabilities perfectly. Using every inch of the width of the runway, he began turning the wheel to put the Bentley into a beautiful four-wheel drift. Blackie, who had done a good deal of racing himself, never knew that a corner could be negotiated at such a speed. He watched in amazement as Johnny pulled *Diane* on to the rough, narrow perimeter track.

Blackie did not relax until the car was back safely in their garage, and when he stepped out, his knees felt soft and quite incapable of holding him up. Johnny climbed down from the high seat, stretched, and gave a deep yawn. 'She corners nicely, too,' was all he said.

They walked slowly over to the office together. After a moment's silence, Blackie asked, 'What happened to the Atlantic? I was too busy saying my prayers to notice.'

Johnny twirled his goggles by their strap like a boy with a toy windmill. 'Don't tell me the great Danny Black was scared?' he asked with a grin. Then, while Blackie was still protesting hotly, Johnny added, 'The Atlantic was around the corner and away while I was still stamping on the brake. That's where modern braking really tells.'

'And a lightweight body,' Blackie added. 'There's nothing *Diane* couldn't do if we wrapped a modern tubular frame around her engine and put on discs.'

'Only she wouldn't be *Diane* then,' argued Johnny, who was not going to allow himself to be drawn into a technical argument. He caught sight of Mervyn Williams' broad back as they passed the workshop entrance. 'Hey, Mervyn,' he called out, 'Blackie thinks it's time we jazzed up *Diane*. You know, tubular framing, and alloys and all that tripe people are so crazy about nowadays.'

Mervyn turned slowly and glowered. 'I won't have irreverent talk like that outside my works,' he warned. 'I don't care for it, that I don't.'

'No, Mervyn, seriously now, come here a minute,' asked Blackie. He was usually the first of the trio to discard frivolity. 'I've been having some deep thoughts.'

Johnny mocked, 'Deep thinking's my preserve, Blackie.'

'Deep thanks,' muttered Mervyn as he joined them. 'That's what you should be giving after that ride.'

'Ah, so you saw us keeping up with that Atlantic,' said Blackie. 'I thought I was dreaming for a moment. *Diane*'s got an incredible turn of speed, Mervyn. That was the latest Mark III Atlantic with all the new modifications – disc brakes, 11 : 1 compression ratio, double over-head camshafts, the lot. It was one of their three Le Mans cars –'

'Le Mans!' cried Johnny excitedly, with a sudden springy bounce. 'You mean we should –'

'Yes, why not? Why shouldn't we enter *Diane* for Le Mans?'

A silence fell over the three of them as the staggering enormity of this suggestion sank in. Even the workshop lathe had been switched off by one of the apprentices and there was not a sound in the garage area.

'Le Mans,' breathed Johnny again as an Eastern pilgrim might mutter the magic word 'Mecca'. Le Mans, the world's greatest motor-race, *Les Vingt-Quatre Heures du Mans*, the fantastic twenty-four-hour gruelling grind around the eight-mile French circuit south-west of Paris, where, for many years now, on the second Saturday of every June, men and machines had fought through a day and a night for the highest honours in motor-racing.

Since the revival of the race in 1949, Johnny had driven at Le Mans three times, twice in a Cunningham and once in a French Talbot, before he had fallen in love with vintage cars. Like every great driver he had dreamed many times of flashing past the chequered flag as winner. But Le Mans was for modern sports cars, futuristic cars, too, for factory prototypes were admitted by the regulations.

And now here they were seriously discussing entering their twenty-five-year-old Bentley.

'Madness,' muttered Mervyn Williams. But the other two knew him well enough to know he was thinking nothing of the kind.

'The entry list closed weeks ago, of course,' said Johnny. 'But I know the secretary of the A.C.O. pretty well.' He was referring to the Automobile Club de l'Ouest, which organizes the race. Johnny knew everyone in motor-racing circles; he would pull some strings. 'I'm pretty sure they'd make an exception for *Diane*,' he added. 'So long as she gets through the scrutineering, I reckon they'll take her for old times' sake if nothing else.'

Bentleys had won five times at Le Mans before the war, more times than any other make of car. Four years in succession the handsome green cars had taken the honours, and in 1929 the first four places had fallen to the great make. A Bentley at Le Mans again – that would create a sensation.

'This calls for a tea session,' said Blackie decidedly. 'Harry,' he bawled out to one of the apprentices in the workshop, 'brew up some tea for us, will you?'

They sat on the ground round the petrol can, sipping their great mugs of tea again, Johnny gesticulating excitedly as he discussed racing tactics, Blackie puffing soberly at his pipe – a heavier, more solid figure than Johnny but now almost equally excited at their sudden inspiration; and Mervyn Williams, short and squat in his white overalls, interjecting solemn warnings that quite failed to impress or depress the other two.

'It'll be hard going for the next few weeks,' said Blackie. 'We'll have to work like slaves on the preparation.'

'Who cares if it's day and night work?' said Johnny, 'It's worth anything – especially to see Barnaby James' face when he sees us turn up.'

Blackie had forgotten about the Atlantic competition manager. And of course Atlantics would be their chief rivals among the British machines. Barnaby James would be scathing about their chances – and he could afford to be with his tremendous financial resources. 'Money wins races' was the old truth in competition motoring – and it was at that moment that the awful realization struck the practical Blackie.

He suddenly leaped to his feet, spilling his tea. Johnny looked up in amazement. 'What on earth's hit you?' he asked anxiously.

'We're mad – utterly, completely mad,' Blackie exclaimed. 'Here we are, nattering on and on, seriously thinking about entering a car for Le Mans, and we haven't given a thought to the little matter of cash.'

'Money, money,' grumbled Johnny. 'Why do you always have to bring that up?'

'You ass,' said Blackie. 'It'll cost hundreds. The preparation, tyres, fuel, shipping her and the service van – to say nothing of ourselves – to Le Mans.'

Johnny looked up aghast at this sudden shattering of their dream. For a few minutes they had lived in a wonderful fantasy world, and now everything had fallen apart.

'We'll borrow some from the bank,' muttered Johnny without conviction.

'Don't be idiotic. We're up to our eyes in debt already. No,' Blackie went on gloomily, 'we'll just have to pack in the idea.'

Without a further word Mervyn got up, snorted in disgust at this waste of his precious time, and disappeared into his workshop.

'Better do some letters, I suppose,' said Blackie quietly. 'Do you realize it's three weeks since anyone walked in here, let alone bought a car?'

To sell a couple of cars – or even one of their higher-priced ones – that's all they had to do. That would provide them with the necessary cash. And the only car they could sell was the unique, wonderful *Diane*. 'Ah, it's bitter, that's what it is, bitter,' sighed Johnny as he wandered away disconsolately with a tin of brass polish and a rag to bring new shine to the radiators and lamps of their stock of cars.

He stood for a moment, his hands on his hips, looking at the rows of beautiful vehicles, some of them nearly fifty years old, all of them hand-built by craftsmen who knew and loved their trade. There was not a badly made car among them, and, thanks to Mervyn and his apprentices, they were mechanically sounder than most new cars on the road.

'All dressed up for the party, and nowhere to go,' he thought sadly, remembering the days when they would reckon on selling half a dozen vintage cars a week.

'Johnny, my boy,' he told himself firmly as he sprinkled some liquid on the radiator of a 14–40 Humber, 'you'd better polish up your salesmanship as well as your brasswork.'

Chapter 2

Mike Shows Off His Brakes

'MR WILD, Mr Wild, hey, Mr Wild!' called Harry the apprentice above the roar of the lathe in the workshop. The young lad was half out of the open double doors, beckoning across excitedly to Johnny who was busy staring with blank incomprehension at one of Mervyn's blueprints on the wall.

'What is it, Harry?'

Harry, an eager red-haired youth and a fine precision worker, ran across the workshop. 'It's a customer – at least I think it's a customer,' he said rapidly.

It was Saturday morning. If 'Eds and Vins' was ever to have another customer, the chances were that he would appear on a Saturday morning. Before the slump in vintage cars, they always reckoned on selling a couple of cars on Saturdays.

Johnny tried to appear unimpressed as he combed back his hair, brushed down his shabby blue suit with the palms of his hands, and passed an oily rag across the toes of his old shoes. Johnny believed that technique and presence rather than outward appearances counted in salesmanship.

Mervyn brushed by him as he made his way to the door. 'It'll be a flirt – bet your life,' he muttered gloomily. Johnny prayed that for once it would not be. 'Flirts' – the impecunious motoring enthusiasts who could not resist wandering among their stock asking a lot of questions and wasting time – were the bane of their lives.

The customer did not look hopeful. He was a red-faced young man in his mid-twenties, wearing an old duffle-coat and sporting the longest handle-bar moustaches Johnny had ever seen. He stood beside his beat-up old Beaver Hornet of the mid-thirties, when more trashy sports cars were built than at any other time.

'Good morning,' opened Johnny briskly. 'Hope you haven't come here for some chassisless box on four wheels. If so, you're wasting your time. We only deal in Vintage and Edwardian motors – to use the good old expression.'

The man looked at him rather nervously, and Johnny gave him a critical look back. He always began roughly, then in his own individual manner turned on the flattery. 'Not that you look the undiscriminating sort,' he admitted grudgingly. 'What's your name? Reckon I've seen you at V.S.C.C. meetings,' he added, referring to that sacred body, the Veteran Sports Car Club, in a casually knowing manner.

'Perce Maner,' said the man heartily. 'You're Johnny Wild, aren't you?'

Johnny nodded. 'Ah, Perce Maner, yes, yes, of course,' said Johnny, though he had never heard the name before in his life. 'How do you do, and what can we do?'

They walked off together towards the rows of gleaming parked cars, each with a neat sign made by Blackie giving the price – from £50 to £750. Johnny kept up his own brand of sales talk all the way, talking man to man, enthusiast to enthusiast, showing an astonishing knowledge of each vehicle, including the mechanical specifications, which he had learned by heart from statistics prepared by Blackie on each car as they bought it.

'. . . then, of course, there's this really superb example

of a "Shelsley" Crossley; 15·9 horsepower. Side-valve, four-cylinder job. Ran in the 1914 T.T. Very rare; doubt if there's another in the country. . . . Or this . . .' And so it went on.

At last the man was able to put in. 'I really want something a bit more sporty – something with a bit of guts.'

Johnny tipped his head, heaved up a shoulder, and pursed his lips reprovingly. 'Well, of course,' he said, trying not to wince at the expression 'guts', 'I always say it's the way they do it rather than what they do. Now you can pick up an old Ford V-8 for less than the cheapest car here, but, well, surely *you* know what I mean.'

The man in the duffle-coat was suitably humbled and hastened to reassure Johnny that he was of the Vintage cult.

'Now this 5¼-litre Stutz may be what you're after. Came in fifth at Le Mans – after four Bentleys, of course – in 1929. Quite a motor-car.'

And Johnny, to his own amazement, sold him the Stutz for just £700, after he had firmly indicated to the man that the Speed Six was not for sale.

Johnny refused any allowance on the Beaver. 'What could we do with it? Not our sort of car,' he told him. Mr Maner did not seem to mind, but Johnny was a little surprised when he was asked to throw the thing on a scrap-heap because Mr Maner did not want it any more.

Johnny fingered the cheque lovingly, feeling as though he owned the Crown Jewels, as Mr Maner drove away in the handsome Stutz, his moustaches twitching with delighted excitement.

He was barely out of earshot when Johnny swung

around, raised his arms to the sky, and shouted out with a great bellow, 'SOLD.'

He was doing a war-dance, jumping and leaping about the concrete area between the buildings like a young gazelle, when Blackie and Mervyn Williams, followed at a discreet distance by the apprentices, appeared.

'It's gone,' he called. 'I've sold the Stutz. We've got seven hundred quid. We're off to Le Mans, to Le Mans we will go,' he sang, and threw the precious cheque up into the air, where it was caught by a gust of wind, and driven at last into a puddle.

'You prize clot,' shouted Blackie, retrieving it and dabbing the wet ink tenderly with his handkerchief. Then his face broke into a happy smile. 'Never mind, nice work, Johnny. So we're going to dice with death at Le Mans after all.'

They walked arm-in-arm over to *Diane*, standing as proudly as a prize Alsatian at a dog show, at her appointed position of superiority beside the other cars. They ignored entirely Mervyn Williams' mutter – in which the excitement was scarcely concealed – of, 'Work, work, more work, never a rest for the engineers.'

It meant more work for all of them, but they threw themselves into it gladly. Johnny dealt with the formalities, travelling up to London twice and making several telephone calls to France. Blackie looked after the supplies problem, going out to arrange for the supply of racing tyres for *Diane*, which had long been out of stock at the makers, and bringing home in the back of their little service truck barrels of the engine and axle oil the Bentley would require.

At the garage work went on eighteen hours a day. The

apprentices received their back pay, which cheered them a good deal, and the noble Speed Six became the centre of all their thoughts.

On the following Tuesday morning Johnny took the car out on to the airfield for her first serious testing. The choice of the rear axle ratio was all-important, and this meant many hours of fast motoring with a stop-watch and a keen eye on the rev. counter.

It was almost lunchtime and Johnny had just completed his twelfth run when he spotted again the low shape of an Atlantic leaving the works on the far side of the airfield. He drew *Diane* in to the edge of the runway and watched the sports car approach, viewing it this time with a professional eye now that he knew it would be one of their chief competitors at Le Mans. 'It looks sleek and horribly efficient,' he thought to himself, recalling with respect the great organization, the millions of pounds, and the recent and continuous racing experience that backed up the Atlantic racing team.

The car blipped down into second and then braked at the end of the runway. Johnny examined the driver closely, trying to identify him beneath his helmet and goggles. But it was not until the driver opened the little door, threw back his goggles, and stepped out that Johnny, with a start of surprise, recognized who it was.

'Mike,' he called joyfully, 'what on earth are you doing in that tin squib?'

Mike Corrigan strolled across the gap separating the two cars with the characteristic rolling gait that Johnny remembered so well from the old days, grinning happily.

'Nice to see you, Johnny,' he said. 'And why are you taking the air in that souped-up old truck?'

'And, having got over the pleasantries, tell me your news,' Johnny asked.

Mike Corrigan swung himself up on to the spare wheel of the Bentley, moving with loose-limbed effortlessness, and sat astride, looking down at Johnny. 'That'll be easier if you'll kindly silence this ancient pumping engine, which is also shaking my spine to pieces,' he said.

The pulsating beat died as Johnny switched off, and conversation became easier.

Mike Corrigan, a lean, wiry Irishman, smaller than Johnny but with the same tough physique, was an old friend of the vintage trio. Mike had fought in the same squadron with Johnny and Blackie during the war, and they had gone into the motor business together after they were discharged. They would have been working together now if Mike had not married; with a wife and a rapidly increasing family, he reluctantly had to leave the uncertainties of used cars and take an appointment as a test driver with the Atlantic organization. It was four years since they had last met, and Johnny had no idea that Mike had transferred to Barnaby James' Competition Unit.

'That's better,' said Mike. 'Now we can talk. I heard a funny story last night,' he went on, looking at Johnny craftily out of the corner of an eye. 'Somebody told me you were entering this hulking old grandfather for Le Mans. Of course, I roared with laughter and told the body that Johnny Wild had a great sense of humour and was always pulling people's legs. "A twenty-five-year-old Bentley at Le Mans," I told him. "Don't make me laugh."'

Johnny looked up at him calmly. 'Well, I will make you laugh,' he said. 'Though you may laugh out of the other side of your face when *Diane* beats the Atlantic team home by a healthy margin.'

Mike leaned forward with a serious expression and

spoke earnestly to Johnny. 'Look, Johnny, we're old friends, and you won't mind a few home-truths. You live in a sort of fantasy vintage world of golden sunsets where everything stands still. You never see anything of modern motoring. I've been with Atlantic for a long time now. They've got teams of research engineers who compile this much data every working day' – and he stretched his arms wide apart – 'production planners who turn out five thousand cars a week, each one ten times more reliable than the best of your vintage stock.'

'Mass-produced, shoddy tin boxes,' interrupted Johnny, 'without an ounce of soul or character. I'd like to see what an Atlantic looks like when it's as old as the newest car in our stock. A little pile of rust.'

'Oh, Johnny, you're so emotional,' sighed Mike. 'The Irish are supposed to be sentimental, I know, but for lack of realistic balance, you English take some beating. I like vintage cars, too, as you know from the old days. But they should only be a hobby – not a business. And as for racing vintage cars against this modern stuff – well . . .' And he shrugged his shoulders helplessly. 'Don't you realize, he went on, 'that our smallest family saloon can outpace anything you've got – more quietly and on half the petrol?'

'Except *Diane*.' Johnny put in firmly.

'Well, yes, I suppose so,' Mike conceded reluctantly. 'But as for putting her seriously up against that,' he said, pointing across to the gleaming Mark III Atlantic Sports, 'well, that is a bit daft. For twenty-five years since your beloved Bentley was built – and I do agree she's a noble-looking old beast – thousands of motoring engineers from Detroit to Tokyo have been *improving* the internal-combustion engine and its chassis. And *Diane* doesn't have one of those improvements.'

'What you forget, Mike, my lad,' Johnny said cheerfully, 'is that W. O. Bentley was more than twenty-five years ahead of his day when he designed this engine.'

There was a moment's silence between the two young men. Both were motorists, who lived for cars and fast driving; they were old friends who had shared the dangers of wartime flying, but their two philosophies were a world apart. Nothing either of them said, Johnny realized, would convince the other. There was no need to worry – unless, of course . . . 'Mike,' Johnny asked seriously, 'are you one of the Atlantic team drivers at Le Mans?'

Mike nodded and then gave Johnny the old, familiar grin. 'That's one reason I'm trying to change your mind. I know what these Mark III's can do. And I know what a terrific team manager Barnaby James is.'

'As a team manager, yes,' agreed Johnny, but decided not to say more out of respect for Mike's loyalty to his boss. He had met Barnaby James several times, and what he had seen he had not cared for. He was glad that he was not working under him, but then that was Mike's business.

Mike swung off the wheel of the Speed Six and lit a stubby black cigar. Johnny remembered that Mike always liked to begin any fast motoring with one of these evil-smelling things clutched between his teeth. 'Well, I still think you're daft, and you'll be the laughing-stock of the racing world, but I know you're the most obstinate old stick-in-the-mud that ever got behind a steering wheel. So here's to Le Mans,' Mike said with a short laugh and a wave of his arm. 'And if you last out to the first pit stop, I'll treat you to a bottle of champagne – you'll need it.'

Johnny swallowed his retort and watched Mike climb into the Atlantic's driving seat, adjust his goggles, and start up. 'See you in la Belle France,' he shouted to Johnny above the noise of his engine.

The Atlantic shot away, the wheelspin stirring up a mass of loose stones like a burrowing dog and leaving twin blue scars of burned rubber on the tarmac. To Johnny's surprise, Mike took the Atlantic on to the perimeter track that encircled the entire airfield. It was rough going and there were frequent curves and several sharp corners. This clearly was not a high-speed test. Johnny had heard that the Atlantics were having trouble with their rear suspension, which was based on an adapted form of the De Dion layout. Mike must be testing the result of new modifications, Johnny decided.

Mike had always been a fine, steady driver, and Johnny watched with admiration as he pushed the little car to the limit on the bumpy loose surface, holding her beautifully on the corners. For a moment the Atlantic went out of sight beyond the brow of the slight hill on which the airfield had been built, then it appeared again, going very fast on the other side. Two more sharp corners, for which Mike changed to second, then with a rising scream the Atlantic was tearing back towards him to complete the first lap.

Johnny knew it was bad policy, but he could not resist it. Mike's cracks at vintage cars had nettled him. 'I'll show him *Diane* isn't outclassed,' he muttered, pressing the starter and slipping the car into gear.

As the Atlantic flashed past, Johnny let in the clutch, and the big car roared away in pursuit. Mike did not realize that there was a challenge on at first, and Johnny was close on his tail before he was spotted in the Atlantic's rear mirror. Then Mike raised an arm in mockery, put his foot down hard, and settled to some really fast motoring.

Johnny pulled the gear lever into top, put his right foot hard down, and the gap between the two cars closed.

Three laps they made like this, both drivers fighting with the steering on the rough surface, Mike struggling to throw off the big green car from his tail, Johnny – as calm as if he were a chauffeur driving a limousine around Hyde Park – holding his own with the low, flying silver machine.

Then slowly but surely the Atlantic began to draw ahead. On the short straights Johnny could hold it comfortably, and there was nothing to choose between their respective acceleration. But on the corners it was a different story. Even though he made his changes and stamped on the brakes at the last possible moment, the light weight and superior disc brakes of Mike's car allowed him to keep his foot down a fraction of a second longer at each corner. The most skilled driver in the world could do nothing to offset this disadvantage, and Johnny wisely decided to retire from the unofficial race before his weakness became obvious to the canny Mike.

He drew in *Diane* at the entrance to the garage, and watched Mike go past once more. Then he drove slowly into their yard. 'This is a serious business,' he thought to himself. 'If a few laps of the airfield can show up her brakes, what's twenty-four hours on the twisty Le Mans circuit going to do?' He switched off, and answered his own question gloomily: 'It's going to leave us on the starting line, that's what it'll do.'

Magnificent though they had been in their day, Johnny had always known that by modern standards *Diane*'s brakes would be her weakest component in serious competition. The Bentley was more than twice

the weight of any sports car built today, and her braking
system was a quarter of a century old.

Johnny climbed down from the driver's seat and
patted the Speed Six lovingly. 'We'll have to get Dr
Mervyn Williams to fix you up – and fast,' he added.
'We've less than three weeks to give you something that'll
make you stop as fast as you go.'

He walked over to Blackie's office to report progress
on the morning's testing. But his friend met him on the
way, looking serious and forbidding.

'What's up?' Johnny asked. 'Did you see that performance with the Atlantic?'

'Oh, forget about the Atlantic,' Blackie said irritably.
'Forget about your testing and Le Mans, too. That
cheque's bounced.'

Johnny halted in his tracks, dumbfounded and
appalled by the news. 'Bounced?' he said unbelievingly.
'You mean that moustachioed old phoney was a crook?'

'Yes – we're one Stutz and £700 down. The bank's
just called up and told me the cheque's been "referred
to drawer."'

A sudden burning rage against Mr Perce Maner and
his sharp dealing died as quickly as it had flamed up,
and Johnny was left with nothing but flat depression.
Even if they found him, the most they were likely to
retrieve was their car; and they had plenty of cars, but
no money.

'Oh, Blackie, I'm sorry,' Johnny said contritely.
'Taken for a mug – and if anyone was a mug I thought
it was him.'

They had always accepted cheques without question
in the past and had never been let down, and it was
usually possible to trace customers if there was any
trouble. But everything was false about their Mr Maner

– name, address, cheque, banker; and probably even those terrible moustaches, thought Johnny miserably.

'Never mind, Johnny,' said Blackie, patting him on the shoulder. 'We're only back where we were on Saturday morning. And we weren't too miserable then.'

'Steady old Blackie,' Johnny grinned wryly. 'Don't know what we'd do without you.' And that's the truest thing you've said today, Johnny decided. For four years his sure hand had steered their vintage garage through crises, cheering them when they were in low water, planning and striving to get them back on an even keel, and restraining their enthusiasm and extravagance when they were riding on a wave crest of prosperity.

'Of course it may be a blessing in disguise,' Johnny murmured. 'I had a little dice with an Atlantic – driven, believe it or not, by Mike Corrigan, who's joined Barnaby James – around the airfield just now. It was quite a scrap while it lasted, but poor old *Diane*'s brakes,' and he sighed. 'Dear, oh, dear!'

'Mike took you on the corners, did he?' asked Blackie.

Johnny nodded. 'Perhaps he was right, old Mike, when he said we were daft thinking of Le Mans.'

Blackie grunted agreement as they went together into the office. And it is doubtful if two people have ever passed through a door in such a state of complete disbelief in what they said and what they heard.

Somewhere at the back of Johnny's mind there had grown in the past few minutes a hard core of determination that he would drive at Le Mans that year in the Speed Six. Johnny's courage, drive and ambition had brought him first past the flag in a dozen *Grands Prix* and thirty-five major sports car events since the war. It was not only on the racing track that Johnny Wild disliked being baulked. . . .

Chapter 3

Barnaby James Noses In

IT was an odd thing because neither of the other two knew that Johnny had a great-aunt. But the telegram on the breakfast table clearly said: DEEPLY REGRET THAT MABEL WILD PASSED ON PEACEFULLY YESTERDAY STOP COME AT ONCE. And it was signed by a firm of solicitors in Kidderminster.

'Poor Great-aunt Mabel,' murmured Johnny. 'One of the best she was, too. As it's "at once" I'd better take *Diane*.'

He swallowed a cup of coffee and waved good-bye to Blackie and Mervyn. 'Be back by supper,' he told them.

They heard him start up the Speed Six in the yard below and tear off down the main London road.

'Poor Johnny, he's quite heartbroken,' said Blackie.

'Don't see what the rush is if she's dead,' muttered Mervyn without looking up from his newspaper.

Johnny reached his destination in half an hour. But he was not at Kidderminster, which was one hundred and forty miles from the garage. Instead, he steered *Diane* between the ancient, decaying pillars of a lodge gate and drove carefully up a long drive between old beech woods, across a deer park, through a double avenue of magnificent rhododendrons and azaleas, and finally on to a broad sweep of gravel in front of a great Elizabethan country house – Limborough Park, the seat of the eighth Duke of Bucks.

Johnny parked *Diane* alongside another car, a car which for sheer grace, beauty of line, and general air of distinction closely rivalled the Bentley.

The car was a 1911 Rolls-Royce Silver Ghost tourer, one of the finest remaining examples of Sir Henry Royce's masterpiece – a car which embodied the mechanical perfection of a genius with a finish in every minor detail that has never before or since been rivalled. Standing there in the early morning sun, it looked like a duke's carriage – as indeed it was; or one of his forty-two carriages. For the Duke of Bucks was not only a connoisseur of the vintage and Edwardian motor-car; he had the means to indulge his passion, and owned one of the finest collections in the world. He had bought a number of cars from Johnny in the past, and they were old friends as well as fellow-enthusiasts.

A touch on *Diane*'s horn brought the Duke out through the massive iron-studded front doors, putting on his deer-stalker hat with one hand and carrying a bag of tools with the other.

'Johnny, my dear fellow, how very good to see you,' he called out cheerfully. He was dressed in knee-breeches and a tight-fitting tweed jacket with eight buttons down the front, and had the general air of an aristocrat whose world had stopped the day Edward VII died.

'Good morning, your Grace,' Johnny greeted him. 'I trust you are as happy and bright as the morning.'

'Can't grumble – can't grumble,' the Duke said, lifting up one side of the Rolls' bonnet. 'A little plug trouble in the Ghost, that's all. Come and see.'

Johnny looked over his shoulder into the spotless interior. Not a trace of extraneous oil or dirt was ever allowed to mar the outside or inside of any of the Duke's vehicles. 'Looks all right to me,' said Johnny cheerfully, 'but then a sort of haze gathers over my mind when I look at an engine. Can't think how anybody invented the thing. It's all I can do to understand a Watt beam engine.'

The Duke pushed home the plug spanner and began turning. 'Can't appreciate the real beauty of these cars unless you know something about their insides.' He straightened up and suddenly looked anxiously and intently into Johnny's face. 'You haven't reconsidered, have you, by any chance?' he asked, giving a little nod of respect to indicate *Diane*.

Johnny glanced at the kindly old Duke, whose expressive face was screwed up into lines of anxiety. 'One of the best' was his oft-repeated and characteristic description of the Duke of Bucks. And it was as true as it was brief.

'Well, I *have* come over to talk about *Diane*, though the other two think I'm at the bedside of my deceased Great-aunt Mabel, whoever she may be.'

The conversation continued in the delightful Silver Ghost, the Duke saying that he always preferred to talk while he was driving. The engine was started simply by manipulating the ignition up and down its quadrant from advance to retard – a unique feature of old Rolls-Royces – and then they purred along the drives of Limborough Park at walking pace in high gear, with no sound whatever beyond the crunch of the tyres on the gravel.

'You don't really mean, my dear Johnny, that after all these months of persuasion you are going to let me buy the Speed Six?' asked the Duke.

'Well, sort of,' began Johnny awkwardly. For once he was thrown off his balance and did not know quite how to begin. The Duke had no idea that the garage was flat

37

broke; *Diane* was the only car they had in stock that the Duke wanted, and he did not want to give the impression that he was begging for a loan.

Johnny explained carefully and slowly (for the Duke was rather deaf) about their plans for Le Mans and how they had decided that the Speed Six really did stand a chance against the best that the opposition could put up, about the run with the Atlantic which seemed to prove this, and finally, and as delicately as he could, that they would need a great deal more money than they possessed to enter the car, and, as an additional expense, to do something drastic to the braking system.

The Duke listened carefully, nodding his head from time to time as he steered the Silver Ghost sedately through the park. He turned the car around at the top of a rise, and they drifted down between an avenue of great elms, planted by the third Duke in the eighteenth century, back towards the elegant mansion.

'This is great news, Johnny,' the Duke said soberly. 'By George, that magnificent brute should be able to show her heels to these aerodynamic whippersnappers they call sports cars today.'

'What I'd like to suggest, your Grace,' Johnny went on hastily, 'is that we should sell you *Diane* at the last price you suggested – just a thousand pounds, I think – but that you should pay us now and take delivery after Le Mans.'

The Duke thought this over for a moment while Johnny waited anxiously, hoping that the Duke would not think he was taking advantage of his longing to add the rare Bentley to his collection.

The Duke glanced at Johnny for the first time since they had set out. 'And if she is wrecked in the race?' he asked; then added with a smile, 'They do sometimes, at Le Mans, you know.'

The Duke of Bucks and Johnny Wild had done a lot of business together over the years, but always happily and with complete understanding. Johnny was an honest businessman at any time; and with the Duke he had always been completely frank and open.

'That's your risk,' he said soberly.

'I thought so,' said the Duke after a moment's silence. 'And it's a risk I'm prepared to take. What's more,' he went on, accelerating the Rolls-Royce briskly, as though carried away by the memory of the dust-ridden, hazardous Gordon Bennett races of his younger days, 'if you get *Diane* over the line first at Le Mans and prove to the world that the old cars are still the fastest as well as the best, I'll pay you another thousand. Not just to celebrate,' he added in a more business-like tone, 'but because she'll be worth at least that much more if she carries that honour in her records.'

A great glow of satisfaction and excitement filled Johnny as he watched the Duke step down from the Rolls and trot across to the Bentley. They would have enough money now, *Diane* would be at Le Mans, after all, and though it would break their hearts to see the wonderful car go, she would at least be in good hands, and she would have her last magnificent swan-song in France, the spiritual home of motor-racing.

After allowing the Duke time to run his hands lovingly over the car he had wanted more than any other for so long, and after the usual tour around the Duke's stables, filled with his priceless, gleaming collection, Johnny climbed into *Diane* and started up.

'One last thing, and very important it is, your Grace,' said Johnny, to the Duke, who could not keep his eyes off the green Speed Six. 'Please don't, on any account, say anything to the other two about our deal. It might take their minds off the race,' he added craftily.

The old Duke smiled conspiratorially. 'Not a word,' he confirmed. 'So long as you ensure that my car performs creditably at *Les Vingt-Quatre Heures du Mans*. I shall be there to see that she does.'

'Trust me,' called Johnny with a laugh as he let in the clutch and revved up.

And the Duke doffed his deer-stalker and gave a little bow to *Diane* as she roared off down the ancient gravel drive.

'You could knock me down with a fan-belt,' exclaimed Blackie in amazement. 'Dear old Great-aunt Mabel.'

'Yes,' said Johnny again, 'every penny of it to me. I never knew the old girl loved me so much.'

Even Mervyn, curled up in the corner chair in their living-room with a bright and breezy book called *Magneto Maintenance: An Advanced Treatise*, looked up and nearly smiled. 'It's back to the old grind on the Bentley tomorrow, then,' he muttered. There was a pause for the oracle to speak. 'Disc brakes may be the answer,' he said, still without looking up. 'Self-adjusting, of course. And we'll have to make them up ourselves. They don't make them big enough for *Diane*. Anyway, I want to make some mods. of my own. May do the trick, though it's doubtful.'

Barnaby James turned up at the garage a week later, in characteristic fashion, with a scream of tortured tyres and trailing a cloud of blue exhaust smoke. It was well known that in his rough hands no car lasted longer than three months.

Blackie looked out of his office window at the dusty

red machine parked in their yard, and thought how fortunate it was for Barnaby James that he did not have to buy his own cars. Then, wondering what the Atlantic number-one driver could want with them, but determining to be cautious with their wily opponent, Blackie went out to greet him.

Johnny had *Diane* out on test that morning. Mervyn had had the head off the engine, giving it a scrupulous cleaning and polishing, and had fitted and ground in new valves with ultra-strong springs to cope with the new loads and sustained high revs *Diane* would be called on to take. Johnny had been taking it gently, watching his instruments with minute care, and was in the middle of the runway when he saw Barnaby James' red Atlantic streaking along the road towards the garage.

'And what's that old snake after?' he wondered. Johnny was inclined to take a less charitable view of his fellow-men, and was more inclined to doubt their motives, than Blackie. What was more, Johnny considered Barnaby James a phoney – though he had to concede that he was a magnificent driver – and he had no patience with insincerity.

He turned the Speed Six towards the garage and cruised slowly along the runway. 'I'll bet he's come to tap us for information about *Diane*,' he thought to himself. 'Hope to goodness Blackie keeps his mouth shut and the two boys don't chatter.'

When he arrived in the yard Johnny saw Barnaby James and Blackie in earnest conversation by the Atlantic. They both turned when they saw him, and Barnaby James moved curiously towards the Bentley.

'Mr James has come over on a very generous mission,' Blackie called to Johnny. 'He's very anxious for our welfare.'

'Oh?' remarked Johnny. 'That's very good of you, Mr James.'

He put out his hand to their visitor, and felt a warm, damp, soft one in his own. Barnaby James was dressed as carefully as always in a tight single-button lapel-less jacket, tight artery-stopping trousers, calf-high black Italian boots, and a quarter-inch tie. The whole ensemble caused Johnny to avert his eyes in horror.

Barnaby James took off his smart bowler in greeting and revealed a carefully brushed head of bright red hair. His smooth, chubby face beamed in delight at Johnny's words.

'Not a bit, old man. Wouldn't like to think of a fellow-sportsman getting into trouble. Wouldn't be the thing, old man.'

'Trouble?' asked Johnny curiously. 'What sort of trouble, Mr James?'

'Well, I hear you're entering this dear old thing' – and he gave a high-pitched, indulgent laugh and glanced at the Bentley – 'for Le Mans. I thought it was one of your little jokes at first, but now I gather the A.C.O. are being sporting and that you're thinking of it seriously. Speaking as man to man, if you know what I mean, I think it would mean a lot of trouble to you. Trouble financially, old man, and trouble on the track.'

He turned to Blackie to include him in the conversation. They both stared at him silently, only just able to control their annoyance. 'You know what the Sarthe circuit's like. Pretty crowded with sixty cars on the line. I'm afraid you might find yourselves, well' – and he gave a little cough – 'rather likely to baulk the faster cars.'

Blackie saw the signs of anger on Johnny's face and gave him a warning frown. 'Oh, I don't know about that, Mr James,' Blackie said hastily. 'It's not like the old days at Le Mans now. The road's pretty wide, you know.

42

I think there'll be plenty of room for you to pass.'

Barnaby James did not have a very subtle mind, and he missed the sarcasm in Blackie's remark. 'Yes, yes, old man, I reckon the Atlantics'll be able to cope. I'm only thinking of you. A joke's a joke and all that, but I think it'll wear a bit thin after a few laps.' He gave another high-pitched giggle. 'Wouldn't want you boys to be the laughing-stock of the racing business, you know.'

The smooth, chubby little man wandered slowly round the Bentley, and Johnny noticed that, though he was smiling and chattering casually all the time, his keen blue eyes were darting over the front and rear suspension, and, most carefully of all, at the big-drummed brakes.

'Now, I'm a sentimentalist myself,' he was saying (and Johnny decided that that was the year's most whopping lie), 'and I've a soft spot for these fine old cars. I can understand your feelings, old man. But I'm a realist, too. Have to be in this game. And, you know, the last Speed Six to run at Le Mans lapped at barely 90 m.p.h. back in 1930. And the lap record's up into the 120's now.' He shrugged his shoulders and treated them to a wry smile of pity. 'Figures speak for themselves, eh?'

But they were not going to allow themselves to be drawn into an argument. That would be playing straight into Barnaby James' hands. Why should they point out to their rival that in those days the Sarthe circuit was a narrow, twisty, ill-surfaced road with corners that could not be taken at much better than 25 m.p.h.? Above all, why should they draw attention to the fact that Mervyn Williams had received delivery only the day before of a set of special triple Weber down-draught carburettors and that in the workshop they were already completing a set of disc brakes to their own design?

'Yes,' agreed Blackie, 'figures speak for themselves,

Mr James.' And because it was clearly what Barnaby James wanted, and no harm could come from showing him the unmodified Bentley power unit, he raised *Diane*'s hood and revealed the gleaming interior.

Barnaby James muttered, 'Thanks, old man, very good of you,' and buried his head deep inside. 'Ah, purists, I see,' he said at last. 'Loyal to the vintage cult – and quite right, too. She's just as she left W. O. Bentley's loving hands a quarter of a century ago.' He seemed relieved, and his broad, charming smile revealed a double row of pearl-white teeth that would have been a credit to any film-star.

'Well, my good fellows,' he said, wiping his hands on a spotless silk handkerchief, 'if I really can't persuade you that you'll be wasting your time and your money taking this dear old-fashioned lady to Le Mans, then I suppose I'd better be off. Plenty to do across the way. We're getting an extra 25 b.h.p. out of the Mark III this year. I think we've got the race pretty well in our pocket, eh?'

Blackie gave a sigh of relief. He had noticed Johnny's look of suppressed fury, and it was obvious that he would explode in a torrent of abuse at any second.

But they had not got rid of the smooth little man yet. He paused as he walked past the workshop, listening to the whir of the lathe and the steady whine of an electric drill.

'Haven't seen that eccentric old mechanic of yours for some time. Mind if I blow in?' And before they could stop him, he was half-way through the open doors.

But that was as far as he got. Standing squarely in the entrance, hands on hips, and a massive wrench protruding prominently from his overall pocket, was Mervyn Williams.

44

'Morning, Mr James,' said the Welshman dourly, and there was no smile of welcome on his face. 'What can I do for you today?' He moved firmly across to bar his way in.

'I'm on a goodwill mission, this morning,' Barnaby James told him glibly, and gave a little laugh.

'Goodwill? Goodwill, Mr James? First time I've heard that word used in connexion with your activities. Spying mission's what I'd call it. And you won't be putting your rubbery little nose in *my* workshop, that you won't, man.' Mervyn Williams was well known for speaking his mind.

'You mustn't take any notice of our Mr Williams,' Blackie said apologetically as Barnaby James leaped nimbly into the Atlantic's driver's seat.

Barnaby James let forth a falsetto laugh and smiled at Blackie, not in the least put out by his reception. 'No need to apologize, Mr Black. I know Williams. Got a heart of gold really. Let him have his little secrets, eh, old boy?'

The red car jerked forward and tore out on to the main road without a pause. Johnny and Mervyn watched it from the workshop entrance, muttering furiously together.

'If *Diane* throws a piston and has four blowouts, I'll still lick that oily little snake around Le Mans,' promised Johnny.

Anger usually broke Mervyn's silent contemplation. 'You wait till I get those Webers on – and those brakes. Then you'll show them what modern engineering can do to an old thoroughbred,' he told Johnny grimly. He shook his fist after the rapidly disappearing Atlantic and turned back into his workshop.

Chapter 4

A Saboteur Pays a Call

'TOMORROW and tomorrow and tomorrow,' quoted Johnny, 'creeps in this petty pace . . .' He gritted his teeth and for the twentieth time that morning pressed down with all his strength on the brake pedal, and *Diane* came to a screaming halt.

'Phew, petty pace indeed!' he muttered. 'Never mind, heigh ho for Le Mans tomorrow.'

He had been hard at it since seven o'clock, up and down the runway, testing Mervyn's disc brakes. Twenty times he had taken the Bentley up to 100 m.p.h. and then mercilessly stamped on the brakes. With no previous experience to work from, they had had to start from scratch, and on that first run Mervyn had only theoretical figures to assess the likely disc temperature.

The heat generated by a single brake application at 100 m.p.h. is tremendous. One of the great advantages of disc as opposed to orthodox internally expanding brakes is that they generate far less heat, and because they are exposed to the air, lose it more quickly. With a machine twice the weight of any other in the race, the heating problem was even more critical, and Mervyn, therefore, had secretly had made to his own design a water-cooling system for each disc, fed from a central reservoir well away from the engine and kept just above freezing point by a minute electrical refrigeration device.

It was on this – as much as the new carburetion – that they were depending to give them efficiency at least equal to that of the Atlantics and the foreign entries at Le Mans.

Mervyn was beside the car in a flash, the temperature-recording apparatus in one hand. This he placed in turn against each of the brakes, recording the figures in a little book.

'Any sign of fade yet?' he asked Johnny.

'Only from my right foot,' complained Johnny. 'And from the tyres, I should think. They must have about faded right away.'

'They'll take a worse beating than that on Saturday,' Mervyn muttered, busily examining his figures. Which was true enough, for between the long straights at Le Mans are the Esses, Tertre Rouge, Mulsanne, and Arnage, all cruel to a car's brakes for twenty-four non-stop hours.

'Good,' said Mervyn at last. That was all, but it was all Johnny expected as confirmation that their engineer was satisfied. He had never in all his racing experience driven with brakes like these. Each time they had pulled the big car up smoothly and dead straight, and they had been as good at the end of the gruelling tests as they had at the beginning. Johnny now felt confident of holding on to the tail of any Mark III Atlantic.

'Why don't you let me give you a lift back?' asked Johnny. 'Just to celebrate.' They were in the centre of the runway, and Mervyn would have a good mile and a half's walk back to the garage.

But Mervyn glowered, muttered, 'Got more respect for my neck than some,' and set off across the grass with his instrument and notebook, his back slightly hunched as if in disgust at the idea of tearing around in a racing car.

'Odd, very odd,' considered Johnny for the hundredth time. 'Superb pit manager, supreme genius at

47

making cars go fast, but prefers his own two feet. Feet indeed!' murmured Johnny, who considered them best suited for use on motor-car pedals.

A telephone call from Dover came through to them on that last evening. It was from Mike Corrigan; and Blackie left the supper table to answer it.

'Hullo, Mike,' answered Blackie cheerfully, and the other two looked up from the table in surprise. 'Thought you'd be across the Channel by now,' for they had all watched the procession of service trucks, caravans, and trailers carrying the Atlantic team pass along the road that morning.

'Yes?' said Blackie after a moment's pause. 'Yes?' he said again, more anxiously. 'But what do you mean, Mike?'

They could just hear the hollow, distorted sound of Mike's voice from the earpiece across the room.

'Can't you tell us any more?' Blackie asked urgently. But there was a sudden click, and the phone went dead in his hand.

Blackie replaced it slowly on its cradle and returned to the table looking puzzled. 'Don't get it, don't get it at all,' he told Johnny and Mervyn.

'What did he say?' Johnny asked.

'Hardly sounded like Mike's voice at all,' Blackie told them, 'though it was a bad line. He talked very quickly, and his voice kept fading away almost – almost as if he was turning away half the time. As if he was looking over his shoulder expecting to be interrupted.'

'But what did he *say*?' asked Johnny again, more irritably.

Blackie pushed away his half-finished meal. 'He said he wished we weren't coming.'

'That's natural enough. None of us likes being in rival teams.'

'Yes, but it was the way he said it. And he said this year's Le Mans was especially important to Barnaby James, because there's a directorship waiting for him if he wins – and the sack if he doesn't.'

'That doesn't surprise me either,' said Johnny, 'after last year's disaster when they all retired from overheating in the first hour. The management at Atlantics is a tough crowd of tycoons, and they must have spent a quarter of a million getting this year's cars and team ready.'

Blackie stood up and filled his pipe. 'Look, I don't want to be melodramatic, but Mike wouldn't go to the bother of telephoning unless he had something pretty important to say.'

'You mean it was some sort of warning?' asked Johnny.

'Ah, there's a bright lad,' said Blackie, smiling for the first time since the telephone had rung.

Johnny got up and slammed his chair forcibly back against the table. 'There's nothing I'd like better than a spot of fun and games with Barnaby James,' he said grimly. 'Calf-length Italian boots indeed!' he added in disgust, as if anyone who affected such footwear stood small chance against the muscular, wiry Johnny Wild.

Less than twelve hours later they began to understand just how anxious Barnaby James was about the Bentley's competition, and also that his methods might be more subtle than they had given him credit for.

They were taking the mid-morning boat from Dover, and by seven o'clock Blackie and Mervyn, with the help of their two apprentices, had got most of their stores aboard their little service truck. The four sets of special racing tyres were the last to go in, and they were all piled up in a neat stack at the back of the truck.

Blackie was about to slam the doors shut when he noticed a small dark mark on the side of one of the tyres. He rubbed it with his finger, bent down anxiously, and looked at it closely.

'That's a nasty fault,' he muttered. 'Not like Sureflows to let that pass. Lucky I ordered an extra set. Look at this, Mervyn,' he called. 'A hole clean through the cover, just as if someone's drilled . . .' His voice faded away in horror.

Blackie frantically pulled the tyres off the stack one by one, running his hands around the walls of each in turn, and then heaving the tyre aside with a gasp of dismay. Drilled neatly through the side of each, evenly spaced a foot apart, were a dozen or so one-eighth inch holes.

Mervyn, standing beside him now, met his eyes. There was no need for either of them to put into words the meaning of this catastrophe. Sureflows kept no stock of racing tyres for Speed Six Bentleys; there had been little demand for them for twenty-five years, and Blackie had had the utmost difficulty in persuading them to hand-mould these four precious sets of high speed tyres for Le Mans. Moreover, they had already left their departure for France very late. . . .

'Johnny,' Blackie called urgently, 'come here and look at this. We're done for now.'

Johnny left the Bentley and ran across to the truck. 'What's the matter?' he asked anxiously.

'Sabotage,' said Blackie in a flat voice. 'Someone must have broken in last night – someone who knew about our arrangements in detail.'

Johnny examined the ruined tyres in turn. 'Someone who's mighty anxious to stop us,' he said quietly; and

Blackie noticed that the hand holding the tyre was shaking slightly.

Johnny walked silently, and with the curious stiffness of controlled rage, across to the wooden building which they used for their stores. Blackie saw him running his fingers along the window-sill, examining the frame for signs of a forced entry, then heard him call out, 'This is the way they came in, all right. A child of four could have broken in. What a bunch of fools we are!'

Blackie, Mervyn, and the two young apprentices were sitting on the ground, four broken spirits, staring at the wreckage of their plans, when they heard Johnny's voice on the telephone in Blackie's office. 'A week?' he was saying, 'No, a week's no good. We've got to have them by tomorrow midday at the latest.'

There was a pause while the man at Sureflows explained the utter impossibility of meeting the order; and then Johnny said curtly, 'I'll be over in an hour, and I don't want any argument. Those tyres'll be ready tomorrow morning if I have to make them with my own hands.'

Johnny appeared from the doorway and leaped down the steps. 'We'll get those tyres all right,' he told them determinedly, 'I'm off to Sureflows to see to that. Blackie, you get on to Dover, will you, and tell them we're not sailing this morning. We'll have to fly across tomorrow afternoon.'

'O.K., I'll fix that,' said Blackie, matching Johnny's sudden sense of urgency.

'Scrutineering at Le Mans finishes at six o'clock tomorrow,' Johnny reminded them as he jumped into *Diane*. 'And we'll be there, don't worry.'

They would have to be if the Bentley was to run in the great race. The Le Mans regulations were as strict as

51

military discipline; in 1954 the entire Italian Maserati team had been eliminated because they were a few minutes late for the scrutineering.

Mervyn Williams watched gloomily as Johnny drove away. 'Huh!' he grunted. 'He's got a hope.'

At well-ordered staff work Danny Black was unsurpassed. And at twelve o'clock precisely on the next day a somewhat battered ex-Silver City freighter touched down on the runway behind their garage.

But it is doubtful whether Blackie could have handled the manager and technicians at Sureflows with the furious determination Johnny applied, and which, within an hour of his arrival, had infected the staff with an enthusiasm as great as his own. Work went on throughout the night, just as if the reputation of the great factory depended on *Diane* being on the starting line at Le Mans. And soon after the freighter had taxied up to the back of 'Eds and Vins', Johnny roared through the gates with the back seats of the Bentley piled high with thirteen new racing tyres.

An hour later Johnny dropped into the pilot's seat of the freighter, which he had insisted on flying himself. Looking back through the cabin door, he could see the big green Bentley in the fuselage, firmly roped down and looking rather like a large dog in a kennel too small for him. Beside their little service truck, sitting about on cans of oil, brake fluid, wooden boxes of spares and tools, were Blackie, the two apprentices, and Mervyn Williams who strongly disapproved of air travel and had insisted on bringing with him assorted air-sickness pills and several huge overcoats as if he were prepared for open-cockpit flying.

'O.K.?' asked Johnny with a grin.

Blackie waved a hand in acknowledgement. 'Take it easy, Air-ace Wild,' he called.

'My co-pilot'll see to that,' and he glanced across at the displaced captain in the other seat. 'Here we go, then.'

The engines roared into life, and Johnny, with the sure ease of three thousand hours' experience, taxied the freighter out to the end of the runway.

Chapter 5

Race Day Draws Near

ABOUT the entrance of the garage in Le Mans where the scrutineering of the cars took place, a large crowd of motoring journalists, race enthusiasts, and small boys had gathered. For the past few days the teams of racing cars had been arriving in varying degrees of secrecy at the French city – from Italy, from Germany, from England and the United States, and from the factories of France itself, which had built the winning car in seven earlier Le Mans races.

The scrutineering – the minute examination of the racing-cars by the officials of the A.C.O. to ensure that they met the stern regulations of the race – was the first chance the crowd had to see at close quarters the sixty or so cars that would be on the starting line on Saturday.

Blackie and Mervyn, who had come straight from the airfield to watch the arrival of the teams, had seen the wicked-looking, red Italian Rampinis drive up under their own power, each with a pair of dark-skinned mechanics lolling casually on the tail, smoking cigarettes. The deep snarl of their exhausts sounded impressive, they were known to be very fast – and Italian cars had won before. There was some doubt about their reliability, and their pit-work – like all Italian pit-work – was inclined to be excitable. But, as Blackie had remarked to Mervyn, 'You've got to hand it to those Ities, they know how to prepare a car.'

Three teams of baby French cars had followed, contenders for the small-car class award and the Index of

Performance handicap prize. These miniature wonders, with smooth, low aluminium bodies and weighing less than half a ton, could lap Le Mans at 85 m.p.h. and reach well over 'the ton' – the magic 100 m.p.h. – on the Mulsanne straight.

As they rolled one by one into the garage, a bearded man in a beret standing next to Blackie said in French, 'Maybe our country can't produce big fast cars any more, but nobody in the world can touch our babies.'

'*Ça c'est vrai*,' murmured Blackie, whose French was not very good.

A deep murmur of heavy diesel engines had heralded the approach of the German Stuttkas. There were three of them, ugly, savage-looking machines, with all-enveloping, polished alloy bodywork, each one astride its own trailer, each trailer as spotless and gleaming as its charge, and capable, it was whispered, of 100 m.p.h. fully loaded.

The crowd watched in silent awe as the trailers drew up beside the kerb and the mechanics in clean white overalls, who had been standing at their positions like firemen on an engine, leaped down and, in perfectly disciplined order, ran the Stuttkas down their ramps and into the garage.

'They're going to take some licking,' thought Blackie. 'Those Germans are certainly efficient, and the Stuttkas look faster than ever this year.' With the Atlantics, they were the warm favourites for Le Mans.

The three American Crawley Specials followed, arriving under their own power and in the charge of the American millionaire sportsman, the popular Ed Crawley, who answered the call of welcome from the crowd with a cheerful wave.

'You'd think they'd run away with the race with

those massive 5-litre engines,' Blackie whispered to Mervyn.

Mervyn shook his head. 'Engine capacity doesn't count for everything,' he answered. 'It's weight distribution and suspension that Ed Crawley never seems to get quite right. Don't know why.'

It was true. An American car had never won at Le Mans, although the Americans had had the fastest cars in several races. Experts had put forward many reasons for this, but it was simply because their power units were tuned and developed stock engines and were not – as were the European engines – designed especially for high-power sports cars. The drivers and team managers also lacked experience of Continental road-racing, and for this same reason – in reverse – European cars had hardly ever figured prominently at Indianapolis. It was a matter of understanding your own racing better.

But there was no doubt that Ed Crawley, with his lovely sleek Crawley Specials in the American national racing colours of white with twin blue stripes running down the centre of the machines, was the most popular driver. The French love a trier, and Ed Crawley had tried year after year, and had come within an ace of victory.

'Here comes Barnaby James,' warned Blackie. 'Let's get out of here for a bit. I don't trust myself any more when he's around.'

They caught a glimpse of his bare red head in the leading car, smiling for the photographers and waving a cocky arm in greeting. Then, before Mike came into view in the second machine, they were around the corner.

Ten minutes later they came running back at the sound of a great cry from the garage entrance. They guessed that the welcome was for *Diane* – and there she came in wonderful dignity along the narrow, cobbled street, like an old duchess arriving at a palace.

Some of the young boys were laughing, for the Bentley contrasted strangely with the modern, low bodies of the other cars. But what *Diane* lacked in smoothness she made up in stark purposefulness. There were no frills about her appearance, everything from the solid-looking P100 headlamps and stone guard over the radiator to the tough, semi-elliptic rear springs being unashamedly exposed.

Everyone was talking as Johnny, matching his driving to the tone of the car, brought her gently up to the garage and cleared the plugs with one last mighty roar from the engine. '*C'est magnifique.*' '*La Belle* Bentley!' came the comments from every side. 'Wonderful old cars,' commented the motoring editor of a London daily paper. 'I remember when Barnato and Birkin and Kidston and the other Bentley boys brought the green cars to Le Mans in the late twenties. No one could get near them in those days.'

'Don't give him any chance now, though,' said his companion. 'Out of date – right out of date.' And the editor agreed sadly.

Johnny nodded to the other two, and they joined him inside the garage, where a team of French officials under a supervisor were waiting to check the Speed Six. They were an efficient, unemotional body, and the only comment about the old car was, 'It's a long time since we had one of these here.'

Then with Johnny, Blackie, and Mervyn watching anxiously, they set about *Diane* like a team of doctors examining a patient before an operation. Lamps O.K. Petrol filler-cap correct diameter. Fire extinguisher O.K.

The windscreen wiper was passed, but they were told that an emergency hand operator would have to be fitted before the race. The measurements of the car were taken carefully; and finally, and most important of all, Mervyn was asked to open up the bonnet.

The supervisor took over now, checking every detail of the carburetion and ignition, and ordering the head off the engine so that the cylinder capacity could be confirmed. Six thousand, five hundred and ninety-seven cubic centimetres. Quite correct. 'The biggest engine this year,' commented the Frenchman. He gave a wry smile and glanced along the length of *Diane*. 'And so it needs to be with this body.'

The Bentley had passed with flying colours, even the revolutionary braking system creating nothing more than technical curiosity among the officials.

'Come on,' said Johnny after the formalities were over and they had been handed their stamped forms, 'let's get some practice in before it's dark.'

They got into *Diane*, Blackie sitting beside Johnny in front. 'You'll be there in ten minutes if you come with us,' Blackie told Mervyn. 'It'll take you an hour by bus.'

He shrugged his shoulders and glowered at their smiling faces behind the windshield. 'But at least I'll get there safely, man,' he said, and turned away to find the nearest bus stop.

'One of these days we'll have to strap Mervyn into the back and take him for a short run. It's only like throwing children into the deep end of a pool. They love it when they're in.' And Blackie waved good-humouredly to their engineer as they passed him on the pavement.

Johnny weaved in and out of the thick Le Mans traffic, the Speed Six creating a great sensation among the pedestrians, and the other drivers wherever it went. Like a dog shaking water from its back, Johnny broke free at last from the packed streets, and accelerated with a roar down the short stretch of straight road leading to the circuit.

'Ah, but it's good to see the old place again,' sighed Blackie as the huge grandstands, already flying the flags of the nations, came into view. There was the Dunlop bridge, a great half-tyre built to take the spectators across the road to the inside of the track. And there, beyond the stands, were the dozens of marquees, gay and brightly coloured, set up by the accessory and component manufacturers, the oil and petrol companies, who supplied their products to the racing teams.

'Looks as good as ever,' agreed Johnny as they caught their first glimpse of the smooth wide road, shining in the low evening sun like a great dark-blue river.

Blackie waved their pass at the official on the gate, and then, with a sense of excitement that never lessened with the years, Johnny took *Diane* inside the world's most famous racing circuit.

A gendarme held them up for a moment on the edge of the track as a Rampini shot past in a blur of red, slowed down with a scream of revs for the gentle curve under the bridge, and accelerated away up the slope beyond. A pair of silver Stuttkas followed, running hub to hub in the centre of the track, slowed down together with typical German discipline like a pair of Prussian guardsmen, and snarled away out of sight.

The gendarme waved his baton, and Johnny drove across to the line of pits, which ran like a series of open shop counters on the inside of the track. Above each was painted the name of one of the teams – Crawley, Atlantic, B.R.C., Rampini, Pegoso, and a dozen more, with Bentley half-way along. Here was their headquarters for the battle to come, the brain-cell where their tactics and strategy for the campaign would be worked out, where – until Sunday evening with the race over at last – all their thought and all their labour would be devoted to their charge.

Johnny turned the car around and backed her close against the counter. 'Everyone's here in good time this year,' he said, looking along the irregularly spaced line of a dozen machines on either side of them, each with a pack of greasy mechanics groping about under or inside.

Blackie sat up for a moment on the back of the seat and surveyed the scene. A Stuttka in the next pit roared into life and began revving its engine deafeningly. Blackie held his hands over his ears. 'And this modern tinware makes more noise every year,' he shouted. 'Come on, let's do a quiet lap to see how the circuit looks.'

Before setting off they had a look in their pit to see how the apprentices were getting on with the unpacking. A truck had brought their equipment over from the plane, and the two lads were getting it into some sort of order.

'Good work, boys,' Blackie told them. 'Most important thing is to get those tyres under cover, and guard them like your own life. We'll run on the touring covers tonight. One of you had better be here on guard all the time,' he warned them. 'We're not taking any more chances. And in case of an emergency, produce this and wave it around.' Blackie unlocked a steel tool-box and brought out a Smith and Wesson ·38 revolver. 'It's not loaded so it can't do any harm, but it'll scare away anyone who tries any nonsense.'

Barnaby James looked up from the café table, his

eyebrows raised in an expression of surprised welcome. 'Well, look who's here,' he said. 'Come and join us.'

After a few practice laps Johnny and Blackie had driven back into Le Mans at midnight for a meal at one of the restaurants whose tables spilled out on to the sidewalk in traditional French style. They had not spotted Barnaby James and his party until it was too late.

Johnny looked down at the dapper figure sitting not a yard away, surrounded by his number three driver, Jon Jeans, his three co-drivers – and Mike Corrigan.

'Good evening, Mr James,' he said icily. 'No, thanks, we won't break into your party. But I'm glad you've had the chance to see that we did arrive, after all.'

It was a difficult situation for Mike, who looked away in embarrassment. But the other faces stared up at Johnny and Blackie, hardly able to conceal their hostility while Barnaby James pretended to look puzzled.

'I don't quite understand,' he said. 'I never doubted that your wonderful old machine would get you safely to Le Mans. You mustn't feel there's any hard feelings between us, old man. Got to stick together, we British, eh?' And he let forth one of his high-pitched giggles that made Johnny want to lay the palm of his hand across his chubby cheek.

'As a matter of fact,' said Johnny flatly, 'we had to hire an aircraft to get us here in time, because some thoughtful British decided to ruin all our precious racing tyres at the last minute.'

Barnaby James took a leisurely sip of wine and met Johnny's eyes with a cold blue stare. There was a moment's heavy silence when the whole packed restaurant seemed to be as hushed as a Western saloon in a movie when the hero walks in. Then he spoke quietly, and there seemed to be real concern in his voice. 'I say, old man,' he said, 'that was rotten luck for you.' He looked around at his companions. 'How about a toast to better fortune for the old Bentley?' he asked. 'Raise your glasses, chaps.'

Johnny and Blackie, looking tired and dirty and out of place in their crumpled old clothes, watched the six glasses of wine raised in their honour towards them. Five of the smiles were sour with danger; only in Mike Corrigan's was there a trace of friendliness – and to confirm their impression, their old Irish friend treated them to a slow, conspiratorial wink.

'Thanks,' said Blackie. 'I don't think we shall have any more "bad luck." We know how to look after ourselves pretty well.' They nodded curtly, and drifted back into the thick crowds wandering along the sidewalk.

'That man's a constant threat to my self-control,' murmured Johnny. 'But one of these days my resistance is going to crack – and I'll find myself in jail for assault and battery.'

'It doesn't make it any easier to know that he's going to eat a seven-course dinner and retire to a luxurious suite in the Hôtel Metropole,' added Blackie bitterly. 'While we make do with an omelette and settle down in a sleeping-bag in the tent.'

Unlike the factory teams, who came to Le Mans with all expenses paid, they had to exist on a shoe-string budget. Le Mans in race week was the most expensive town in the world, and they had to watch every penny.

For an hour the two young men wandered through the seething town, along the brightly-lit boulevards, in and out of the noisy, smoky cafés and restaurants and hotels, listening to the chatter of this packed mass of humanity that for these few days talked and thought of nothing but motor-racing.

The words and phrases spun about them like snow on a windy day – 'Throttle linkage cracked . . .' 'Took Tertre Rouge too fast . . .' 'The Stuttkas are getting 285 b.h.p., I hear . . .' 'Spun round like a top . . .' 'Changed the plugs, but she was still running roughly . . .' 'Cracked the bank at Mulsanne . . .'

'Compression ratio,' 'cylinder head,' '125 m.p.h.,' came the technical jargon in half a dozen languages.

'Talk, talk, talk,' sighed Johnny. 'No one on earth talks like racing maniacs. Let's sit down and eat.'

So they found a small and comparatively quiet restaurant in a side-street, and picked up a couple of old newspapers. But every page was covered with pictures of the cars, pictures of the drivers, pictures of the track, and articles speculating on the chances of the various teams.

'Here, take a look at this,' said Johnny, sitting up in surprise. 'They've even got *Diane* in here.' And he passed over his paper with a double centre spread headed in black type, 'RETURN OF AN OLD FRIEND TO LE MANS'.

Blackie glanced at the big photograph of their Speed Six, with Johnny sitting upright at the wheel, driving in for the scrutineering. '"A 6½-litre Bentley, carrying the British racing colours, is a surprise last-minute entry for Saturday's great race!"' translated Blackie slowly.

'"Many old sentimentalists will be glad to see again the fine old car, which last won in 1930, back on the Sarthe circuit. But we cannot help feeling,"' went on Blackie indignantly, '"that this is the joke of the year. No expert rates this ancient vehicle with any chance at all, and its presence on the track may well be a danger to the faster cars . . . !' ' '

'Well, of all the – !' exploded Johnny, digging his fork angrily into his omelette.

It was a trying evening for both of them, and they now wished they had stayed behind in the pit with Mervyn. As a final test of their endurance, a man leaned across from the next table as they were about to leave, and asked them in English:

'D'you hear they've got an old Bentley in this year? Bit of a joke, eh? Some romantic old codgers driving it, I suppose.'

The famous White House, set on a double bend that brought every car down to 90 m.p.h., flashed into the line of *Diane*'s headlamps. Johnny snapped the gear lever down to third and went through on a perfect line, just touching the warning line that bordered each bank. He revved up the engine and slipped back into top with a silent, clutchless change.

Ahead of him were the bright lights of the pit area; and as he began to slow down he thought, 'The next time I come up here, it'll be the real thing. This time tomorrow, I wonder . . .'

It was just before midnight on the last practice night. Ever since 6 p.m. Blackie and he had been taking it in turns around the circuit, trying every corner at varying speeds, and with different approaches, noting carefully fixed landmarks – certain pine trees or bushes or marks on the road verge – at which to change gear up or down or begin to brake, noting engine speeds at different points on the winding circuit, learning every inch of the road.

All the other drivers had been doing the same thing

for the past six hours. But now practice was over, and they were coming into the pits for the last time.

An Atlantic shot past, its red brake lights flickering; a little B.R.C. came alongside, its driver waving cheerfully to Johnny. 'Tomorrow we battle for our lives – today we may as well be friends,' the driver seemed to be saying.

Parked alongside the Bentley pit was a big, high, glistening tourer; beside it an old figure muffled up against the cold night air. 'That's nice of the Duke,' thought Johnny as he cruised in with his engine off. 'Come to wish us good luck on the last night. Only hope he remembers his promise not to say anything about our deal.'

Johnny left *Diane* beside the Silver Ghost Rolls-Royce, two strange and incongruous vehicles among the massed rows of low-slung, modern sports-racing cars. He dropped his goggles and helmet into the driver's seat and stepped forward to greet the Duke.

'It's very good of you to come and see us on the last night, your Grace,' he said.

The old Duke's face creased into a smile. 'I hear from your friends that you could do with a little moral support,' he said. 'Mr Black here tells me there's not a soul in Le Mans or on the circuit who'll give you a chance, eh?'

'We don't mind that so much,' said Johnny, swinging his legs over the counter to join them all in the pit. 'But the mockery's beginning to get us down, I don't mind admitting. We've also had to put up with a spot of sabotage, as I expect Blackie told you.'

The Duke nodded his head seriously while they settled around the timekeeper's table in the middle of the room with mugs of tea brought in by Harry. 'I don't see how anyone can do any more harm to you now,' he said, 'though I'd keep a watch on your stores tonight.'

He sipped his tea and offered his tobacco pouch to Blackie before filling his own pipe. Then he looked around at the three of them with his honest old grey eyes. 'Tell me your policy tomorrow,' he asked them. 'Your secrets are safe with me. You know that there is nothing that could make me happier than to see *Diane* take the chequered flag on Sunday.'

Mervyn looked up sharply from the time-sheet he was ruling out meticulously on the table. The Duke met his suspicion with a laugh. He had known the engineer for years and had spent many hours talking engines with him. 'All right,' he said, 'I don't blame you. You should never really allow your strategy secrets outside your own pit.'

'Oh, don't take any notice of our cheerful chief, sir,' Johnny laughed, banging Mervyn between the shoulders. 'Actually, our policy's very simple, isn't it, Blackie?'

Blackie nodded, and wished he had some of the supreme confidence Johnny always managed to find just before a big race. Blackie's role as second string was a difficult one; he knew only too well that, though he was a good steady driver, he possessed none of Johnny's sparkling brilliance, and the responsibility was weighing on him heavily. 'We're taking things quietly at first,' he told the Duke. '*Diane* always takes a little time to get into her stride, and we reckon that the first six hours are going to be pretty hectic.'

'You're right there,' nodded the Duke in agreement.

'It's all a matter of national and personal temperament when you get down to it, man,' murmured Mervyn without looking up from his ruler and pen.

The Duke took the pipe out of his mouth and turned

his attention to Mervyn, glad that he had broken his
silence. 'Meaning, Williams?' he asked.

'Well, sir,' he began in his singsong, gentle voice.
'The Italians are a Latin race. They're easily excited.
You've only to watch their pit-work to see that. Everyone shouting and running helter-skelter for this and that,
losing their temper and calming each other down by
shouting and cursing at the tops of their voices.'

The Duke gave a deep laugh. 'I see what you mean,'
he said.

'They build the finest cars in the world, the Ities do,
sir. And they've some good drivers, too. But they only
know one way of driving whatever,' he added, almost
smiling. 'Flat out they go, flat out all the time.'

'And that's no good for twenty-four hours, eh?' put in
the Duke.

Mervyn nodded sagely, and retired into silence. It was
a long time since he had made such a long speech, and
the Duke had to be content with that, though realizing
suddenly why this odd engineer from the Welsh valleys
was such an astute racing-team manager.

'And the Germans?' asked the Duke, turning now to
Blackie.

'The German Stuttkas are very dangerous,' he pro-
nounced. 'No doubt of that. They're as fast as anything
here this year, and they've got good drivers. But Mervyn
reckons that temperament'll be the leading factor, in
spite of the terrific discipline of their pit control. The
Germans can't bear being behind another car – especially another Italian car – it's their pride. And as the
Italians in their Rampinis are bound to tear into the
lead at the start, Mervyn reckons that the two teams are
going to strip their cars to pieces by ten o'clock in the
evening.'

The Duke – who knew a good deal about racing himself – nodded doubtfully. 'I hope you're right,' he said. 'And Ed Crawley's American monsters?' he asked. 'What do you think about his chances this year?'

'Chance is the word,' broke in Johnny, leaning back in his tilted chair at an alarming angle. 'Poor Ed has had the rottenest luck at Le Mans. It's due for a change.'

'And yet I somehow don't think it will,' said Blackie thoughtfully.

'Ruling out the odds and ends, that only leaves your old friends the Atlantics among the big guns,' the Duke pointed out with a smile.

'Ah, yes, the Atlantics,' said Blackie.

'The Atlantics,' Johnny repeated, pronouncing the word as if it were an expletive. And Mervyn looked up from his work for a moment.

'There I think we're relying on *personal* temperament to help us,' Blackie said slowly.

'You mean Barnaby James' reputation for treating his cars like a starving man with a can of meat – and no opener?'

'Yes,' laughed Blackie, 'and, of course . . .' And he glanced significantly at Johnny.

The Duke rose from the table and carefully placed his deer-stalker hat on his head. He looked down at Johnny, and his face bore the expression of a schoolmaster fondly regarding a brilliant but over-lively pupil. 'You mean there's some temperament under here, too?' he asked Blackie in mock surprise, ruffling Johnny's long black hair.

'Quite a lively temperament,' Blackie assured him with a grin. 'Spiced with anger and served up with determination and a longing to prove the prophets wrong.'

'We have a few little refined tactics, too,' Blackie continued as he helped the Duke over the counter. 'But we won't bore you with the details. You'll see them in action tomorrow.'

'Ah, tomorrow,' murmured the Duke with a sigh. 'What a day it's going to be! Well, my new Bentley boys, drive well and keep the vintage colours flying.' And he shook them each solemnly by the hand over the pit counter, giving Johnny a specially significant look and saying half under his breath, 'I kept my promise, didn't I?'

They watched him drive off in dignified silence in the darkness, feeling suddenly warmed and encouraged.

'It's nice to know,' said Johnny thoughtfully, 'that though there'll be two hundred and ninety-nine thousand, nine hundred and ninety-nine people here tomorrow who don't give us a chance, there's *one* who'll be rooting for us.'

And Mervyn, who was already back at his line drawing and figure-work, muttered, 'He's all right, that Duke.' Which, for him, was the highest praise in the world.

The long hours of the early morning dragged by. The Le Mans circuit, which would soon echo to the shriek of sixty open exhausts, was silent and in complete darkness – except in the Bentley pit, where a single naked bulb shone the night through, and a figure, taking hourly watches, sat alert and watchful on the counter, the great Speed Six on one side, the precious stores of equipment inside on the other.

At half past three the first touches of lighter grey appeared over the pinewoods on the eastern horizon; the dawn of race day at Le Mans was breaking. . . .

Chapter 6

The Opening Round

THE announcer's voice was tense and solemn. '*Dix minutes*,' he said, pronouncing each syllable slowly; and the vast, tight-packed crowds who heard the words from a thousand loud-speakers shuffled uneasily and set up an excited murmuring like a horde of warriors awaiting the enemy's attack.

The track between the grandstands had been cleared of pressmen and mechanics, and the only people around the sixty machines lined up diagonally in front of the pits were the drivers and co-drivers, with the team managers giving last-minute instructions. The cars, gleaming in their national colours in the bright June sunshine, had been placed in order of engine capacity, with *Diane*, green and resplendent, at the head, the 5-litre Crawley Specials next; then the 3½-litre Stuttkas, the Atlantics, the Rampinis – and far away, beyond the thirty or so 1½- and 2-litre machines, the baby French cars.

'*Cinq minutes*.' A uniformed official marched self-importantly down the centre of the track, clearing away everyone but the drivers who were to take the first spell at the wheel.

Johnny tossed a last kiss with his hand towards Blackie and Mervyn and called out cheerfully to their retreating backs, 'Hope you remembered to put in some petrol.' He switched on *Diane*'s ignition and put her in first gear; then, swinging his goggles and helmet nonchalantly in one hand, he wandered across the track to the little circle marked out for him in white paint on the other side.

The 'Le Mans style' start, imitated all over the world, begins with the drivers sprinting across the road and leaping into their machines. It is the fairest way of spreading out a packed field on a narrow track and is one of the most exciting sights in the world.

Johnny did not usually suffer from pre-race nerves. But no driver could remain unaffected by the tension built up during the final hour, and as the last few minutes ticked by he felt a flutter of mixed dread and excitement, and a longing for the race to begin.

From where he stood close to the protective barrier he could see the heat-waves dancing on the concrete roofs of the stands above the solid mass of white faces that made up an audience twenty times the size any actor had played before. Along the skyline the flags and bunting drooped limply in the still air. Everything now was still and quiet. The wind had died – as it always died for the start at Le Mans.

'*Deux minutes.*' The voice echoed metallically above the grandstands and enclosures.

Johnny wished he had brought darkened goggles. The sunlight was intense, reflecting blindingly from the white concrete and dancing gaily over the massed flowers above the pits, the marquees of bright blues and reds and yellows on the rise beyond, and floating plumply a hundred feet above them, the purple balloon advertising a make of tyres.

'*Une minute.*'

The drivers were standing in their circles now, slowly putting on their helmets, strapping them under their chins. A girl photographer in bright slacks ran along the top of the barrier, snapping her camera at intervals and evading the arms of the gendarmes. The crowd gave a little cheer which was broken by the voice on the loud-speakers again. Thirty seconds to go. Twenty seconds. The big hand of the clock above the scoreboard had almost covered the '12' mark.

The revered and ancient figure of the President of the A.C.O. walked slowly on to the track, carrying the starting-flag.

Johnny slipped on his leather-palmed driving gloves and leaned forward in a slight crouch ready for the get-away. High up in the grandstand behind someone coughed. It was the last sound before the patter of racing footsteps on the macadam as the drivers sprinted for their machines.

Suddenly, in one great blast of sound, sixty powerful engines burst into life. Johnny had thrown himself into the driver's seat, and in one movement let out the clutch and pressed the starter.

The line of cars shot forward irregularly, swinging in and out, swerving and dodging, streaming away up the track in a great milling torrent of raucous, ear-splitting sound. A gust of fume-laden air rose up, and as the cars shot past out of sight they left behind a blue cloud of mixed exhaust smoke and burning rubber.

Before he was under the Dunlop bridge, the three red Rampinis had shot past hard on each other's tails, and a silver Stuttka was closing in on each side of the Bentley. Number 8 Atlantic, Barnaby James at the wheel, was close behind, and when the Stuttka had moved ahead, Johnny eased over to the right to let him go by. As always at Le Mans, the first lap was going to be a wild free-for-all.

At the top of the hill leading down to the Esses, all the big cars had gone by, just as Johnny had planned, and behind him were roaring up the first of the 2-litre machines, headlamps flashing in warning.

Johnny brought back the gear-lever into top, and put his foot down. Ahead of him was a short, downhill straight packed with cars with red lights flickering as they began to brake for the vicious double corner. Down to third again, then into second – heeling-and-toeing both changes.

Hard left into a slight drift, and almost at once hard right again. Up into third, a few seconds in top along the densely wooded straight towards Tertre Rouge. This was a ninety-degree right-hander, with a high bank of soft, protecting sand on the outside into which at least three cars would probably plunge before the race was over, the drivers frantically – and usually unavailingly – attempting to dig themselves out.

For a moment it looked as though it would claim a victim on the first lap. Johnny saw a Stuttka and a Crawley Special race up to the corner ahead of him side by side, the German car trying desperately to get by on the left. The Crawley went through on a beautiful line on the inside, the tail of the Stuttka began to wag dangerously, the driver lost control, and the car spun around through 360 degrees, sending up a flurry of sand, and stalled half-way across the road.

Johnny jammed down hard on the brakes, a Pegoso fell back on his left, and he saw an official leap down from the bank waving a yellow flag – 'Danger: be ready to stop.'

The Stuttka's engine had been restarted and the car was already moving forward as Johnny went around cautiously, hugging the right-hand bank. They were running abreast down the slope on to the long, fast Mulsanne straight, and Johnny could not resist answering the German challenge by putting his foot hard down.

To the other driver's surprise, he could not hold the old Bentley's acceleration in the lower power range, and the Stuttka began to fall behind. 'Come on, then,' Johnny laughed to himself, raising his left arm in the traditional 'Clear to pass' signal. The Stuttka closed up, Johnny shifted into third and surged forward again. But he still had a reassuring reserve of power in hand when the other car crept slowly by at 145 m.p.h. opposite the Hippodrome café a third of the way along the straight.

'She's sounding sweet,' thought Johnny as he listened to the crisp, healthy roar of *Diane*'s engine building up her revs. 'Stay like this, my love, and you'll see us through the twenty-four hours – and maybe catch some of that mad, flying tinware ahead.'

There was a wonderful feeling of relief and freedom on Mulsanne with the straight ribbon of road ahead and the flat, open fields or woodland clear of all spectators, on each side. For nearly four miles he kept the rev. needle steadily at just under the 4,000 r.p.m. mark. It was a strong test of disciplined driving with more speed available at a touch and a dozen cars ahead of him; but Johnny, with his years of experience, knew how to resist temptation, and kept *Diane*'s surging power in check.

Mulsanne corner. It was a near-hairpin once – in the days when Bentleys reigned supreme at Le Mans. But it had been smoothed out over the years, widened and resurfaced, and the obstructing trees chopped down. The other cars were streaming around nose-to-tail as Johnny touched the brake and felt the sure, even tug of Mervyn's discs grip the wheels of the Bentley. Down into third, then second at 45 m.p.h., and Johnny went round as smoothly as a ball in a bearing, safely clear of the bank by six inches. Once again the thunder of the Bentley's exhaust boomed out deeply, and in dignified contrast with the screaming crescendo of the other machines' acceleration.

And there, within a few seconds, was the warning sign for the Arnage corners. Johnny kept a steady distance behind the last Stuttka, and went through the first and second corners a hundred yards behind it. They were among the pinewoods again, and the packed lines of spectators were hard against the barriers.

Arnage. A white ambulance tucked away in an opening on the outside of the corner. A blur of blue-uniformed figures standing prepared for the worst as he went through. Then the blue strip of gently winding road rising uphill towards the double bend at White House.

Already the towering grandstands were in sight over the brow, a vast ocean of shimmering cars in the parks on the left of the track. The flags were waving about triumphantly in the breeze now, the bright colours of the marquees, the flowers, the absurd lolling balloon, contrasting strongly with the sombre darkness of the pinewoods behind.

'First lap,' Johnny said to himself. 'First lap – and all's well.' The first of how many laps in this most gruelling of races? A hundred? Two hundred, if *Diane* stuck the pace. Perhaps nearer three hundred. Over 2,500 miles. Clear across the Atlantic Ocean in twenty-four hours. It was certainly a *Grand Prix d'Endurance* all right. . . .

In the Bentley pit Blackie leaned out anxiously across the counter, stop-watch in hand. Four minutes before the roar of the cars had died slowly away like a receding storm, only the sudden scream of top revs as they changed down for Tertre Rouge a mile away across the woods being heard above the excited murmur of the packed spectators.

During that brief, empty pause, as the cars were fighting it out on the first lap, the track between the grandstands had seemed strangely bare: a hundred thousand spectators – and nothing for them to see.

Everyone had suddenly tensed as the race commentator broke into the silence. '*Au Café Hippodrome, la première* . . .' came his flat voice, bringing news from Mulsanne, where number 11 Rampini, the champion driver Bordoni at the wheel, had a clear lead of four seconds over the second Rampini.

Blackie strained forward to catch a glimpse of the red Italian cars as they came up from White House. There were two machines, running hub to hub, two dark dots that grew and took shape with amazing rapidity. But they were not the same shape; one was a Rampini, all right – and then the word flashed round, thousands of voices exclaiming at once in those few seconds.

'Well, I'll be . . .' began Blackie. 'Mervyn, it's an Atlantic up there with the leader! What a pull-up!'

To slash the Rampini's lead to nothing on the first lap was an incredible feat. But one of the Atlantics had done it. Who was it? Barnaby James, Jon Jeans, or old Mike himself?

Blackie held his breath as the two cars tore up, neither giving way an inch at the approach to the grandstand area. To get around the right-hand bend at the end of the straight it was necessary to brake after the pits.

'It's Barnaby James,' shouted Blackie above the shriek of the two straining engines as he caught a blurred glimpse of the number 8 on the bonnet. 'And he's not slowing down, the fool!'

Both the red Rampini and the green Atlantic held

their top speed right to the end of the pit area, and it did not seem possible for either of them to get around. But it was the Englishman who held out longer; the brake lights of the Rampini flashed first by a fraction of a second – and Barnaby James on the inside got around under the Dunlop bridge half a length ahead, a telltale trail of blue smoke from the tyres measuring the strain he had put on his machine.

Packed close behind came the Crawleys, the other two Rampinis just ahead of them, two of the silver Stuttkas, Mike's and Jon Jeans' Atlantics nose to tail, the third Stuttka – and then with a deep bellow, the dark green Bentley came pounding up from White House like a gallant old war-horse, bearing the number 1 proudly on her exposed radiator.

'Four minutes thirty-five for the standing lap,' announced Mervyn as the Bentley roared by with Johnny sitting up, relaxed and well away from the wheel, in the driver's seat. He entered the time in neat figures on the lap chart, and then stood beside Blackie at the counter watching the smaller cars flash past in little groups of twos and threes, each struggling to break free and get on to the tail of the car ahead.

There was nearly half a minute between the leading Atlantic and the last of the 750 c.c. French cars; and soon the pack would be so spread out that there would be a car in sight all the time from the grandstands.

'And here comes the first lame duck,' said Blackie, pointing down the track to a single machine that was stuttering up the slight incline, trailing a cloud of blue smoke. 'The Pegoso's had it.'

The Italian car, the first of the many casualties that Le Mans would claim this year, dragged itself into its pit and was met by three anxious mechanics. The bonnet was lifted, and when the cloud of smoke had drifted away across the track, Blackie could see the pit-manager bending over the engine. Before the leaders came around again on the second lap, the Pegoso had been wheeled away sadly to the 'dead car park', behind the pits. Twenty-three hours, fifty minutes to go; fifty-nine cars left in the race.

By the tenth lap Le Mans had settled down into a sort of wild rhythm. The drivers and their cars had got into their stride after the mad, whirlwind opening. Right up in the front the dice of the year was taking place, with Barnaby James, driving like a savage demon, holding off the Italian Rampini challenge by less than five seconds. Just behind, the three Crawley Specials were running like clockwork, coming around within a second of their scheduled time on every lap; then, spread out more widely after nearly a hundred miles of racing came Mike Corrigan's Atlantic, the three Stuttkas, and half a mile behind Jon Jeans' Atlantic. All the smaller cars had been lapped, several of them twice, while all down the line little private duels were being fought out for class leads.

The clock above the scoreboard showed five to six when Mervyn Williams ordered Harry the apprentice to get out the signals. 'We'll give him one more lap, and then get him moving,' he told Blackie.

The Atlantics would be coming in for fuel in another twenty-five minutes – Mervyn's neat figure-work gave him that information. Now was the time to put the first of their plans into action. The regulation stipulated a minimum of 280 miles between refuels, so all the cars would be coming in between 6.15 and 6.45. This period would end the first and most important phase of the race, when drivers would change, race managers would be taking stock of their position, and the pundits in the press-room would begin making prophecies and cabling them to papers all over the world.

Mervyn had reckoned that at this critical time they should strike a mortal blow at the leaders – and at Barnaby James in particular.

Johnny was ready for the signal when it came, giving the thumbs-up sign of acknowledgement when he passed his pit. The black diagonal line on a white background with the figure 3 alongside was the code symbol for 'Faster. The next car is three minutes ahead.'

'At last,' he sighed in relief. 'Now *Diane*, my love, let's show them.' The prearranged order had been given: he was to catch the last of the Atlantics – if he could – and pass it before it came into the pit for refuelling. This was the sort of situation Johnny enjoyed.

He settled himself more comfortably into the driver's seat and prepared for some serious driving. He had been using the throttle sparingly up to now; but at the crest of the hill leading down to the Esses he put his foot hard down, feeling the response from the Webers, and went storming towards the double bend with the new exhaust note booming in his ears.

Diane's new urge carried her through the Esses faster than at any time during the race, her racing tyres protesting at the sudden new strain thrust upon them. Three small cars fell behind on the short straight to Tertre Rouge, and Johnny caught and passed a Pegoso just before he spun *Diane*'s wheel hard into the right-hander.

Accelerating away on to Mulsanne, Johnny felt the back of the seat pressing hard and satisfyingly against his back. The needle swung steadily round the speedometer dial – 90 m.p.h. in third, the rev. needle well past the red line; 110, 120, 125 m.p.h. The hedges and fields were a dull blur on either side. The white Hippodrome café shot past. One hundred and forty on the clock at last, for the first time since the start. One hundred and forty-five m.p.h. came up more slowly; *Diane* was nearing her limit, already travelling far faster than her original designed speed.

'One hundred and fifty-five m.p.h. – that's about it,' Johnny told himself. 'And not bad, old girl.' His foot was hard on the floorboards. *Diane* was flat out. Johnny felt a sudden rush of pride in the wonderful car. There was no motoring in the world to equal this, he thought – the wind beating like a hurricane against his face, a pair of French 'babies' appearing to jerk backward as he roared by.

Ease off a hundred yards earlier now for Mulsanne corner. Down to third – second – and neatly around in a perfectly controlled slide. This was motoring – this was Le Mans as it should be.

There was Mervyn, a tiny blue figure leaning far out of the pit holding the stop-watch. And next time round he was holding a board with a white '30' on it. He had gained thirty seconds on Jon Jeans' Atlantic on the previous lap. That was fast driving!

Three laps later Johnny thought he could just see the green tail in the distance on the Mulsanne straight. It was perceptibly bigger before it disappeared round the corner, but Johnny knew that he would have to work hard to cut down that lead before Jon Jeans came in.

The Speed Six's engine sounded sweet and healthy, the new downdraught carburettors, the lightened flywheel, and Mervyn's superb tuning were making all the difference. Nor was there a sign of fade from the disc brakes. The water temperature had risen up close to the danger mark, but that was to be expected, and Bentley engines had always run best when comfortably hot.

Sharp, knowledgeable eyes had spotted the Bentley's challenge. Up in the press-box heads swayed from side to side like rushes in a breeze, whispering incredulously into neighbours' ears. 'Notice the old souped-up lorry, Jack? Lapped in 4 minutes 12 seconds that time.' 'See the old Bentley? Stretching her legs a bit.' '*La* Bentley – *c'est merveilleux – quatre minutes* . . .' 'Say, Milt, that ol' jalopy . . .'

But the exclamations were mixed with smiles of scepticism. She wouldn't hold the pace. A flash in the pan, that's all it was.

Mervyn had been watching the Atlantic pit like a hawk. It was a full fifteen minutes before the pit-manager realized that his third car was being challenged. Mervyn saw a sudden bustle of excitement as the Bentley came by and watches showed that the gap was down to less than half a minute. 'Hang up "Point two four",' he ordered Harry. And when Johnny thundered by next time, he saw that on the last lap he had reduced the Atlantic's lead to twenty-four seconds.

But the Atlantic pit had hung up a sign, too. Were they calling Jon Jeans in early to avoid the humiliation of being passed on the circuit?

The answer came just four minutes later when the Atlantic hove into sight from White House and shot past the grandstands without reducing speed, Jon Jeans leaning forward over the wheel grimly as he dragged the last ounce of power from his machine. And already in sight was the big Bentley – not a quarter of a mile behind.

'Good old Johnny,' laughed Blackie in delight. 'I really think he's going to do it.' Mervyn, impassive as a sphinx, entered the time precisely in the little square on his time-sheet. The excitement of the chase never seemed to affect the little Welshman.

Red, green, silver, blue, white – the colours screamed by; and then two cars lifted over the slight hill side by side – one squat and low, the other tall and ponderous. 'He's caught him, by golly he's caught him!' shouted Blackie, jumping up and down like a schoolboy.

The Atlantic, on the far side of the track, was half a length ahead as they went by; but Johnny managed somehow to squeeze that extra ounce of urge before the Dunlop bridge, and, as the two machines screamed out of sight, the Bentley had a clear lead.

For the first time during the race, the French commentator began to show some spirit. 'Here on the Sarthe circuit this afternoon we have just witnessed an astonishing sight. On the thirty-third lap, shortly before refuelling, the old Speed Six Bentley, privately entered, has at last, after a terrific duel, got by one of the latest Mark III Atlantics.' A murmur of amazement buzzed all around the enclosures, silenced when the commentator continued, 'There is no doubt that the Atlantic was running perfectly, and it appears that the experienced driver, Jon Jeans, had orders to press his car to the limit.'

Blackie swung his helmet down from the peg and slipped it on. Goggles, driving gloves, the blue silk scarf he always wore at the wheel. He buttoned his white overall up to his neck. 'Steady now,' he told himself. 'No nerves, Blackie boy. You're taking on a big responsibility – just take it easy.'

Blackie glanced up at the scoreboard high above, and as he watched, 'BENTLEY *Numéro* 1' was switched from thirteenth to twelfth position for the first time since the opening lap. Barnaby James had lost the lead to Bordoni's flying Rampini, and the order read:

1. RAMPINI	8. ATLANTIC
2. ATLANTIC	9. STUTTKA
3. RAMPINI	10. STUTTKA
4. RAMPINI	11. STUTTKA
5. CRAWLEY	12. BENTLEY
6. CRAWLEY	13. ATLANTIC
7. CRAWLEY	

Behind this mass of heavy metal ran the two remaining Pegosos, and spread well out after two-and-a-half hours' racing, the medium-sized and small cars, which had already lost half a dozen of their number through mechanical trouble.

'Shouldn't take too much notice of that,' Mervyn called out to him. 'There's going to be some juggling around in the next half-hour.'

Blackie nodded. It was true enough. All the cars would be coming in as they were signalled for petrol, oil, and water, and perhaps a check on the tyre tread wear. Precious seconds could be gained, hard-won positions could be lost, by the speed of the pit-work.

'Here he comes,' called Mervyn briskly. He had suddenly become keenly alert, ready for the critical moment ahead. 'Swing out the hose,' he ordered Bert, the second apprentice. 'Oil ready, Harry?' he asked. 'Good. Now this is where your training really counts.'

He leaped over the counter on to the track, waving a white flag to guide Johnny in, calling out loudly over his shoulder at the same time: '*Plombeur, plombeur, venez ici, vite, vite.*'

The *plombeurs* were having a busy time, rushing from car to car to unseal and seal up again the petrol, oil, and water-caps according to the strict regulations, for broken or missing seals meant instant disqualification.

The official was beside him as the Speed Six came roaring up, Johnny flashing her headlights in warning and bringing her neatly alongside the pit with wheels locked in a long slide. Blackie, sitting ready on the counter, watched in admiration; he knew that to stop a racing car in the narrow allotted space among thirty other identical pits after tearing around the track for nearly three hundred miles was a delicate and highly skilled operation.

After the seals had been broken by the *plombeur*, Mervyn and the apprentices pounced on the dusty car, ripping off the straps securing down the bonnet and lifting up each side in one swift movement. Mervyn thrust the nozzle of the hose into the orifice, and thirty-five gallons of high-octane fuel went gushing into the tank. A gallon of oil in the sump. Water to top up the radiator, water for the disc brake reservoir. A swift wipe across the windscreen, the outside rear mirrors. Then tear off the masks over the headlamp glasses, for it would be dusk before *Diane* came in again. This smooth, disciplined pit-work was the fruit of hours of practice – hours that were now saving vital seconds for Blackie.

Johnny sat still, staring dazedly straight ahead for a moment after the car had sunk back on its springs. Then he lifted up his goggles, slipped off his gloves, and wiped his eyes.

'Some dice,' he said laconically to Blackie, and grinned happily through the grime that plastered his face, leaving two white circles where his goggles had protected him from the dust. 'Come on, Blackie lad. Time to toy with death at the gates of hell,' he cracked, and levered himself stiffly out of the driver's seat.

Blackie leaped into the seat and poised a finger over the starter-button ready for the getaway. 'Nice going, Johnny. How's she running?'

Johnny, deafened by the incessant roar of the engine, shook his head and smiled helplessly. 'No ears,' he shouted. 'But if you're asking how she is – she couldn't be sweeter. And the brakes are doing nicely.'

The *plombeur* had refixed his seals and given the O.K. Harry was pulling tight the last of the bonnet straps. Mervyn stood with his hand raised in front of the car; then he suddenly dropped it, and at the same moment leaped aside.

Diane's engine fired at the first touch, and she rocketed away from the pit, her rear wheels spinning as they sought a grip on the tarmac under the sudden impulse of power.

Blackie glanced over his shoulder to see that the road was clear. . . . He was away, in the arena for the second round after a magnificent pit-stop that had cost them just one minute, forty seconds. He knew his limitations, and he knew his orders. He was to do everything he could to hold *Diane*'s position in the race, not to lose Johnny's hard-won place. It was a negative role, perhaps; but with the fastest sports-racing cars in the world and the greatest drivers battling it out in fierce competition it was going to be hard going for the steady Danny Black.

Les Vingt-Quatres Heures du Mans, most unpredictable and ruthless of races, began to cast her first blows as the sun fell below the flat farmland. The finger of chance swung, hovered uncertainly, and finally pointed mercilessly at the Italian cars. They had been driven furiously, with verve and Latin dash, led by the dark-haired young champion, Bordoni, since the flag first fell. The great Tazio Nuvolari himself would have been proud of them.

But a minute error of judgement in the strength of the crown wheel – which had passed all the months of testing and experiment – sealed their fate one by one. Bordoni was the first to suffer. He got only a dozen yards away from his pit after refuelling when the car stopped, and nothing he nor his frantic mechanics could do would transmit the power of those 300 b.h.p. to the rear wheels. The second car was lost somewhere out on Mulsanne. The driver pushed it on to the road verge and began the long trek back to the pits. It was half an hour before the Rampini pit-manager knew he had only one sound car left. It lasted another half-hour, holding lead position against the renewed onslaught of Barnaby James' Atlantic. Then it, too, came in with unhappy sounds from its rear end, and at last joined the other retirements in the 'dead car park'.

Le Mans, notorious for seeking out every hidden weakness in the complex pieces of machinery that fought every year on her circuit, had again upset all the experts' predictions.

The Speed Six Bentley was ninth, Blackie driving the race of his life and lapping steadily at 118 m.p.h. And then drama came again, spectacularly, before twenty thousand eyes down at the Esses. The first of the Stuttkas had had orders to speed up and get past the last of the three Crawley Specials, which were going smoothly in second, third, and fourth positions. Von Reutsch, the German ace, had clipped seconds off every lap for two hours, and was hard on the tail of the American car as they went into the double bend. Hoping to nick past on the short straight to Tertre Rouge, he swung over to the left-hand side of the road as the two cars stormed out of the corner. But for once his judgement failed him, and his front wheel caught the Crawley's tail.

The two cars were on the slowest section of the Sarthe circuit; but even at 50 m.p.h. the results of a nose-to-tail collision can be dramatic. Both cars spun like tops, knocking each other again and again against the barrier with a noise that sent the crowds scattering off among the pinewoods. The Crawley ended up on its side across the road, its oil and petrol from split tanks spreading in a deadly greasy patch over the tarmac.

While the Stuttka limped away with a battered body and a rough-sounding engine, officials raced on to the road, waving yellow danger flags and the red-striped yellow flag which warned of oil on the track.

Bruised and shocked but not badly hurt, the Crawley driver was helped out, and the following cars went by cautiously as buckets of sand were thrown over the oil.

News of the crash came over the loud-speakers a few minutes later. The Stuttka, with a buckled radiator that had lost all its water along the Mulsanne straight, had given up; and Johnny, glancing up at the scoreboard, saw two red lines marked across Number 4, the Crawley, and Number 7, Von Reutsch's Stuttka.

He winked delightedly at Mervyn. 'So Le Mans takes its inevitable toll,' he said in a French accent, imitating the flat, serious voice of the commentator. 'We're running seventh, Mervyn, my lad. And I've never seen Blackie in such good form. Hey, Harry,' he called to the apprentice. 'This calls for a brew of tea. Fix us some good big mugs.'

The only indication Mervyn showed of his excitement was his move from the timekeeping table in the centre of the pit to the counter. He was standing now, leaning out over the track, with stop-watch in one hand and pencil in the other, taking careful notes of the lap speeds of the leading cars. Blackie went by as a blur of dark green in the dusk light; Mervyn snapped the watch, and after a glance at the dial, inserted the figure on the sheet that was now half covered with his neat record of progress.

It was eleven o'clock and Johnny was at the wheel of *Diane* again. With the lights on, Le Mans had been transformed from a brilliant, glittering display of colour and sound and speed, with the hot crowds crushed up against the barriers, to a gay, twinkling fairground. Among the pine trees on both sides of the circuit the cafés laid out in tents were doing a roaring trade in hot sausages, in little paper packets of greasy, crisp chipped potatoes, in succulent, neatly folded pancakes, and dozens of other foods that were washed down with rich red wine. For to thousands of Frenchmen Le Mans is a festival and fair as well as a motor race, and the families of farmers and shopkeepers from the surrounding countryside and towns were out to enjoy themselves. Only the keenest enthusiasts could remain with their eyes glued to the road for all the twenty-four hours, so now – after seven hours of close combat – was the time to stroll in the pine-woods under the lamps strung from the branches, to eat and drink and exchange chatter with friends, to scream about on the dodge-'em cars in imitation of the race running alongside, or to dance under the stars to the music from the loud-speakers.

There would be little or no sleep for the thousands of families in the enclosures that night. Towards dawn some would creep into the close-packed tents erected on the hill above the Esses, others would just lie down on the soft pine needles, like dark cocoons in the shadows, for an hour or two.

All through the long night the cars continued to lap, their speed scarcely diminished in the darkness. '*La ronde impitoyable*,' the French called it. Le Mans is pitiless in its demands; the driver who relaxes the pace falls back instantly, for there are always those behind ready to leap forward at a sign of weakness and take his place. Behind the barriers at Tertre Rouge, at the Esses, at Arnage and Mulsanne, the shriek of the cars rose to a crescendo of sound, died away in the darkness, rose again, and died through the small hours, while the powerful white and orange beams of the headlights swept down the centre of the road, and the cars rushed inexorably by with twinkling bluish-white flashes from their exhausts, like fairy-wands.

There were drivers who drove better in daylight than in the dark; there were others who were happier with the headlights stabbing the darkness ahead; and there were others again who drove equally well in daylight and at night. The old German ace Caracciola and the young British driver Mike Hawthorn were unsurpassed on tricky wet roads, night or day.

Courage, technique, and temperament – and sometimes cunning as well; these were the qualities that achieved victory in the great motor-racing classics. Johnny Wild had them all in abundance, as well as the ability to drive even faster at night. As the two hands of the big clock above the scoreboard closed over midnight, he thundered past between the grandstands – now blocks of brilliant white against the blackness – on the Speed Six's hundred and fifteenth lap. He was full of confidence and was enjoying this race more than any other he had ever driven in. *Diane* sounded as though she could be driven flat out forever without complaining, her brakes were firm, even, and fade-free, he was gaining five seconds a lap on the Stuttka immediately ahead, and – just as they had predicted – the pace was thinning out the field. Another of the Crawley Specials had retired half an hour before with gear-box trouble, after doing six laps in top gear, and Johnny was now lying sixth.

The big headlights picked out the warning sign for Tertre Rouge, the white, intent faces of the spectators huddled close against the barrier, sent a hundred deep shadows of pine trunks scurrying through the woods . . . and then there was the deep protective bank of sand at the corner, a half-buried and abandoned car on its side. Johnny leaned over slightly against the swing of the Bentley, dabbed the brakes, pulled the wheel over to the right, and went around on the limit. Half a mile ahead down Mulsanne were the twin red lights and the short stubby tail of a B.R.C., a scurrying midge in the white beams. He swung out to the left, drew level, and by the Hippodrome café had left it far behind.

Blackie was having a brief doze in the pit before taking over again from Johnny when there was a knock at the rear door. Harry let in a dark, heavily overcoated figure who apologized lavishly for the intrusion.

'My dear Blackie,' said the Duke of Bucks, 'I would never have dreamed of breaking in like this if I had thought you were sleeping.'

Blackie shook himself awake and smiled a welcome to the old man. 'Don't worry, your Grace. Johnny'll be in in five minutes anyway. Bad thing to drive at night with the sleep still in your eyes.'

'I usually reckon on an hour or two at this time at Le Mans, but I can't sleep this year. Too exciting. Far too exciting. Reminds me of the Mercedes and Bentley duel of 1930.'

The two stood beside Mervyn at the pit counter waiting for *Diane* to come around again. 'Let's hope the Speed Six puts up as good a show now as she did then,' Blackie murmured, and at that moment Johnny went by on the brightly lit track, a hand raised in acknowledgement of the pit signal calling him in.

The Duke watched it proudly – the pride of possession mixed with the pride in her wonderful achievement. For years his collector's heart had longed for the unique Speed Six, and here was the car that belonged to him, that was *his* car, showing the world that she could hold the fastest modern sports car built today.

'Ah me!' murmured the Duke, carried away by the emotion of the moment, 'I never thought to see a car of mine in the running for first place at Le Mans. D'you know, young man, the last time I had a winner in a major race was back in . . .' His voice trailed off in horror. What had he said? You ass, you prize ass, he told himself angrily. Now you've given the show away.

He glanced anxiously at Blackie, who was watching him curiously. 'A car of *yours*, sir?' Blackie asked, puzzled.

'Well – well, I mean,' began the Duke, and then gave up. His old face had fallen into lines of worry. Why did he have to talk so much? He ought to have known that if he came to the Bentley pit in a state of excitement he might break his trust to Johnny about their deal.

'I'm afraid I've done a very stupid thing,' he told Blackie and Mervyn, who were listening intently. 'You see,' he said, smiling wryly, '*Diane* is really my property now. What happened was this . . .' And he explained about Johnny's visit to Limborough Park and about the bargain that had been arranged that morning three weeks before.

'The old rogue,' muttered Blackie. 'Great-aunt Mabel indeed! I thought we should have heard before if Johnny had been likely to inherit a thousand pounds.' He was confused and angry, too, even though they had at one time agreed to sell the Bentley to keep the garage going. Then he glanced at the old man, who could understand only too well how deeply they must feel about *Diane*, and was looking worried and sympathetic. 'Oh, it's not your fault, sir.' Blackie reassured him. 'In fact you've been most generous about the whole affair.' He laughed away the last of the embarrassment between them. 'It's up to us to justify your faith in the old car and go on to win – and collect the other thousand pounds off you.'

Mervyn now broke into the conversation, and they both turned to him as he growled, 'You all seem to think we've got this race in our pockets just because we're not actually last and we're still running. You're all daft, that's what I say, all daft. There are five cars, all running well, ahead of us, and we're two laps behind the leader. It'll be a miracle, man, that's what it'll be, if we get the chequered flag.' He glanced down at his stop-watch. 'And what's more, the car'll be in in thirty seconds, and all you can do is natter, natter. Get your helmet and goggles,' he ordered Blackie brusquely. 'And if you don't mind, sir,' he said, stretching out his arms, 'we could do with some elbow room.'

The Duke jumped aside apologetically while Mervyn leaped over the counter with the flag to guide Johnny in. 'And lastly,' he called back over his shoulder, 'if you want to leave us any chance at all, we won't say anything about this so-called deal until the race is over. Quarrelling isn't a help in motor racing.'

His last words were lost in *Diane*'s tyre scream as

Johnny brought her up hard into the pit area, and they were all suddenly drawn into the rush of ordered activity. Front and rear tyre change this time – hydraulic fluid – petrol, oil, and water – brake water reservoir – clean windshield and headlamp glasses. Before the tired, heavy eyes of the spectators in the grandstands, under the white glare of the pit arc-lamps, the dark figures bustled to and fro, knocking off the hubs, rolling away the old wheels, spinning on the new ones. The thick oil glistened momentarily as it drained from the cans in a heavy, even stream.

Blackie pulled down his goggles, gave the thumbs-up sign, and pressed the starter. *Diane* burst into life, anxious, it seemed, to thrust herself forward again like a hound hot on the scent. The headlamps stabbed out as if in sudden warning; the new tyres bit into the asphalt, and the Bentley threw herself forward to rejoin the race.

One-thirty a.m. The music still bellows from the loud-speakers, lost in the exhaust noise as a car goes by and broken from time to time by the commentator's announcements.

A searchlight plays on the fat, lolling balloon, and other searchlights weave lazy, meaningless patterns in the sky.

Only thirty-five of the sixty starters survive now. Barnaby James' Atlantic has a clear two-minute lead over the surviving Crawley Special.

But what is two minutes in twenty-four hours? In 1952 the Frenchman, Levegh, had a big lead over the two pursuing Mercedes with only three hours of the race to run. The crowds were wild with joy, for Le Mans was to be won by a Frenchman in a French car. . . . Then fate struck, as it strikes in no other race, mercilessly and ruthlessly. Levegh, dazed and weary, for he had insisted on driving all the time, engaged first instead of third gear by mistake. The car's transmission could not take the strain, and snapped just past Mulsanne corner; and the gallant Frenchman was out of the race.

La Ronde Impitoyable – pitiless, gruelling Le Mans. . . .

Two a.m. Sensation and sudden disaster. Ed Crawley, in the last of his cars and running regularly in second place, comes up from White House towards the grandstands. He is going very fast, but everything seems quite normal – until just before the pit area his tail begins to swing from side to side, faster and faster. Voices call from the pits, the sleepy spectators suddenly stir in the stands, then hustle themselves to their feet as the American car begins to spin, lurching out of control from the protective barrier to one side to the line of pits opposite.

In the officials' box someone presses the alarm bell before the inevitable crash takes place. For an agonizing second the Crawley is actually travelling backward at more than a hundred miles an hour, trailing a dark stream of burning rubber. . . . One final gyration, and it strikes the barrier in a great flash of flame, spins half a dozen more times like a monstrous Catherine wheel, and finishes up as a blazing wreck in the centre of the road on its side.

Surely no one could get out of that alive. . . . And yet something dark detaches itself from the flames and streaks beyond reach of the yellow, waving fingers even before the firemen have their chemical spraying over the fire.

The popular Ed Crawley is miraculously safe – singed about the face and suffering from shock, but nothing worse. The other cars edge warily past the wreck until it is dragged to the side of the track.

Blackie, back in the pit again, knew that it was useless to try to persuade Mervyn to get some sleep. He sipped his mug of tea – was it the ninth or tenth that night? – and stared at the round, hunched shoulders of the Welshman poring over his charts. They had not exchanged a word for ten minutes, and the only sound inside the pit came from the two apprentices working on a crossword puzzle in the corner.

Blackie yawned and glanced at his watch. It was twenty past two. In the outside world, away from the Sarthe circuit, it was the dead, dead period of the night. . . .

'How's she running?' he asked Mervyn.

There was no answer. He waited until a car went by, and when Mervyn had finished making an entry, repeated his question. There was a long pause, and then, without turning his head, Mervyn said flatly, 'The Stuttkas are losing thirty seconds a lap.'

Blackie leaped to his feet and ran across to the counter. 'What on earth do you mean?' he exclaimed. 'Thirty seconds! *Both* losing thirty seconds.'

At that moment Number 6 Stuttka went by, a silver streak in the bright light, travelling fast, but there was a definite roughness in its engine note.

Mervyn clicked one of his stop-watches and at once looked down at it. 'Well, that one lost thirty-five seconds to be exact, and Number 7 lost twenty-five,' he said.

'But I don't understand it,' said Blackie, still only half-believing. 'How long's this been going on?'

'The last three laps. Both engines are sounding a bit off.'

It could mean only one thing. After less than half distance the pace of the race had now sought out and discovered some weakness in the German power units, and only a miracle could cure the cause now.

Blackie did some quick mental arithmetic. It would take Johnny only just over three laps to catch the Stuttkas at this rate. 'Are you going to speed him up?' he asked Mervyn.

It was up to Mervyn to decide. He was the manager. But it was the obvious move to make with two ailing cars within striking distance – to strike at the first sign of weakness. And Mervyn made it.

'Harry,' he told the apprentice quietly, 'put out the "Faster" sign next time round, will you, boy?'

Johnny responded instantly, clipping another ten seconds off his lap times so that he was past both the two sick German cars within half an hour, and had even knocked a sizeable chunk off the lead of the two Atlantics.

Now it was Atlantic, Atlantic, Bentley. The third Atlantic was trailing twenty minutes behind. Even Mervyn could not resist a show of emotion, though it was nothing more than a nod and a grunt of satisfaction.

Only two Atlantics lay between *Diane* and number-one place at Le Mans. No doubt – like the Bentley – they had a reserve of power to draw on. And their lead was still a substantial one. And yet . . . and yet?

Blackie could hardly credit this sudden stroke of good fortune. 'We've had all the luck so far,' he said to Mervyn.

The little, sad-looking man looked up for a moment from his chart. 'And it's not likely to stay that way,' he said ominously. 'It'll be our turn next – you watch.'

Chapter 7

Flashes in the Night

THE little French boy had called urgently from the door of the Bentley pit, '*Venez ici, monsieur – vite, vite . . .*' and Blackie had followed him out into the darkness, unwilling to leave at this exciting moment of the race but drawn by the mystery and the urgency of the summons. 'At the rear of the scoreboard,' he had been told. 'Please go there quickly, an Englishman wants to talk to you.'

So Blackie had hurried away between the lines of service trucks and trailers parked behind the pits, and waited now in the shadows beneath the high, brilliantly lit scoreboard. 'An Englishman?' he thought to himself curiously. 'What Englishman can want to see me at this time of night? And why so mysteriously?'

He realized suddenly who it must be just before the lean, wiry figure of Mike Corrigan loomed up beside him – an Irishman, not an Englishman, and at this critical moment someone he had no wish to see at all. In fact, so taut were Blackie's nerves from the strain of the race that for one ridiculous moment he thought that this might be a trap, and that the Atlantic team had decided to resort to some rough treatment.

Mike's opening words were hardly reassuring. 'Look, Blackie,' he said quickly, grabbing his arm, 'Barnaby James is out to get you, and he doesn't care how he does it. Your Bentley's not going to be allowed to win.'

'Don't be so daft,' Blackie told him. 'Anyone would think this was a Western saloon roughhouse a hundred years ago, with the sheriff out of town. There are two

thousand gendarmes here, and nearly as many officials –
to say nothing of three hundred thousand spectators to
witness any silly nonsense that rogue Barnaby James
cares to lay on.'

'Not on Mulsanne in the dawn mist,' said Mike – and
then hurriedly pulled Blackie away by the arm. 'Look,
we're too near my pit for comfort. Let's get into the woods
quickly. I'll feel safer there.'

They made their way in silence, keeping a dozen yards
apart, across a stretch of sandy ground, littered here and
there with dark shapes of sleeping bodies under the
stars. They rejoined on the fringe of the pinewoods, and
Mike began talking in a low, urgent voice that com-
pelled Blackie to listen seriously.

'Look, Blackie,' he began, 'you know just how high
the stakes are. Barnaby James is not letting anything get
in his way to win, and he and his cronies know that the
only real threat now is from your Bentley. He came in to
hand over to his co-driver just after me and had a quick
word with Jon Jeans before he went off on his next spell.
There was no time to worry about who overheard – and
I was right beside them. "Get 'im on Mulsanne in the
mist when he comes up astern," he told him. "And make
no mistake about it. Shunt him clean off, and it doesn't
matter if you smash up your car, too."'

'He was still talking to him when he got into the car,
but I didn't hear that bit.'

'That doesn't matter,' said Blackie, thoughtfully.
'That was enough, I reckon.' It was a safe, crafty plan,
almost certain to succeed. Often a thick mist clamped
down over the Sarthe circuit near dawn. Sometimes
visibility dropped to less than a hundred yards, and
along the Mulsanne straight there were no spectators
and only two or three marshals. This was a real threat,

not least because motor-racing is a clean sport and rough-house tactics are almost unknown.

'Thanks, Mike,' added Blackie. 'Nice of you to tip us off.'

It was a difficult position for Mike, for whatever he thought of Barnaby James personally, he had signed up with Atlantics to drive as well and fast as he could and his loyalty must be to that firm. 'You've run a big risk,' he told Mike gratefully. 'You'd better get back or you'll be missed.'

'That's all right. Don't want to see you clots getting hurt, that's all,' he said. 'Take it easy – and see you after it's all over.' He was already moving off into the darkness when he called back over his shoulder. 'I still think you're fools pushing that old souped-up truck around the track, and don't imagine I'm not going to keep ahead of you. You haven't a hope in blazes.' And his familiar, cheerful laugh echoed softly among the shadows as he disappeared. . . .

'So Number 10 Atlantic's to be expendable, is it?' muttered Mervyn when Blackie had finished his story. 'That's their game. Well, we'll see,' and his face set into grim lines.

'What'll we do, warn the marshals?' asked Blackie.

'Don't be silly, man. "Sir,"' he said, affecting a childish whine, '"a little birdie tells us we're going to be shunted by one of those naughty Atlantics." Bah, can't you see their faces? No, Blackie, we've got to be realistic.'

'Looks as though we'd better bring him in then,' Blackie suggested.

'Oh, yes,' Mervyn scoffed sarcastically. 'We'll bring him in and have a chat. There's lots of time. It'll only waste us half a lap, that's all.' He looked down the brightly-lit line of pits to the Atlantic counter fifty yards away. Barnaby James was holding out a sign for the leading Atlantic whose twin white headlamps were tearing up the slope towards them. 'Suffering crankshafts!' Blackie heard Mervyn mutter threateningly 'I'll get even with that low, scheming hound down there.'

Blackie had never before heard such determination in the little Welshman's voice.

And then, for some unexplained reason, Blackie suddenly remembered one of their wartime jokes. Mike had been a party to it, too. It was when they had all three been flying together in the Western Desert on Hurricane fighter-bombers. Johnny had spotted a squadron of Rommel's tanks advancing under cover on to a group of unprotected American trucks. Like most fighter-pilots, Johnny had neglected to keep up his Morse, and all he could remember was S O S – three shorts, three long, and three shorts. For a quarter of an hour he circled low over the trucks frantically flashing the distress signal, to the mystification of the Americans who thought it was Johnny who was in trouble. They even assembled a first-aid party in preparation for his crash-landing, while all the time the tanks were drawing nearer.

The arrival of the rest of Johnny's squadron, who drove off or destroyed the tanks, saved the Americans. But for long after he was known as 'S O S Johnny' and was not allowed to forget the incident. He was also made to brush up on his Morse. . . .

At least, Blackie realized with a start, Johnny would not have forgotten the three shorts, three longs, three shorts. He might even have remembered the complete alphabet. In their kit they had a powerful electric torch.

No good signalling to him from here, he reasoned. A thousand people would see it. Must get somewhere quiet on the track. But there was not much time.

Quickly he dug out the torch and called to Mervyn as he opened the door at the back of the pit, 'I'll get the message to him all right. Back in half an hour.' And before Mervyn could answer, he had disappeared.

The thick pinewoods after Arnage – that was the best place. There was no public enclosure there, no spectators to watch him. Blackie ran like the wind, steering a course across the rough heathland that would keep him clear of the track. He made it in less than fifteen minutes, and lay down gasping for breath in the ditch alongside the road, with the protecting woodland close behind him.

He was on a gentle curve of the track a hundred yards after the sharp right-hander, and could see clear down to the corner. From here he could signal to Johnny as he came round, and, unless there was another car hard behind him, no one else would pick up the message. Lucky I know *Diane*'s shape pretty well, he thought to himself, even if I'm in the glare of her headlamps.

He did not have to wait long. A pair of baby French cars went by, Jon Jeans' Atlantic – the villain of the piece, and lying well back in the field now – one of the ailing Stuttkas, which had already been passed by several 2-litre machines and did not sound as though it could survive for much longer. And then *Diane*.

A chill dampness in the air warned of the mist that would suddenly fall like a blanket over the course, when Blackie picked out the Bentley's deep boom as it braked. There were her headlamps slicing through the undergrowth of the woodland and casting deep black shadows among the pines. Johnny would be down to 40 m.p.h. now, swinging out for the corner.

Blackie caught a brief glimpse of the Bentley's silhouette in the reflected light through the trees, and he lay with his head over the top of the ditch, pointing the torch carefully down the road. *Diane* came around in a perfect line; up into third . . . and Blackie pressed the switch firmly. Three shorts, three sudden flashes from the road verge. Pause. Three longs. Three shorts again.

The Bentley shot past in a holocaust of deafening sound. . . .

Like all supremely good racing-drivers, Johnny kept his mind on the job in hand – constantly and determinedly, for he knew that to relax for one moment when driving all-out on this most tricky of all circuits was to risk, first and foremost, that opportunity of victory; second his machine; and third his own life.

He was through the double twist of White House and heading for the grandstands before he began to realize that there must be some significance in the sudden flashes that had shot out at him from the road verge two miles before.

Three shorts, three longs, three shorts. And his memory swung back for an instant to his old nickname. 'S O S.' The signal had clearly been intended for him. But what on earth could it mean?

Coming out of Arnage on the next lap, Johnny deliberately reduced speed and watched out carefully for the warning pinpoint of light. It came again, from the same spot. S O S, more quickly this time. Then two longs – M, read Johnny, U-L-S-A-N-N-E. His memory of the code was better than it had been back in the war – a fact which was to save his life. As he went past the mysterious signal, only a little more slowly than usual, he just caught the last two letters: B - J.

He hated to be distracted like this when he was driving, especially with the dawn mist coming down fast now. But this was clearly important. He must give a part of his mind to working out the message, and that meant reducing speed. A glance at his pit as he went by showed him the single figure of Mervyn leaning over the counter. There was no sign of Blackie. Could it have been he signalling down at Arnage?

He took the Esses at the speed of a cab searching for a fare, a speed that set the heads wagging at the barrier: 'The old Bentley's packing up at last.' 'Wonder she lasted so long.'

It was the B - J that gave him the clue. Barnaby James' initials. A clear warning linked with his initials must mean real danger, and whatever it was, it would happen on Mulsanne.

'All right,' he thought. 'Do your worst, you slimy old snake. At least I'm ready for you now. What's more, I must have lost twenty seconds working all that out. . . .'

Along the straight out of Tertre Rouge, the first faint shafts of daylight had been blanketed out by the fog that swirled and rolled over the fields and across the track. Driving in the mist and dark at Le Mans called for a special skill and real nerve.

Johnny threw off his goggles that had become smeared with dampness and reached for the visor hanging from a hook on the dash. This he slipped over his head with one hand, and turned his full attention to driving – to driving faster than ever to make up that lost time.

'But I'm a driver,' explained Blackie impatiently. 'A driver, don't you understand? My name is Daniel Black, and I'm one of the Bentley drivers. You must let me get back to my pit.'

'I dare say that is true. Perhaps you are being truthful,' the marshal said unemotionally. 'But not even drivers are permitted on forbidden parts of the circuit. You must come with me to the gendarmes' box.'

It was no use arguing, Blackie realized. He had been spotted as he left the ditch, and now he knew that nothing could shake the determination of a French official – especially one who understood only part of what was said to him – from carrying out his duties.

Feeling like a guilty suspect in a crime case, Blackie walked with the marshal back towards the corner where the gendarmes' post had been set up. 'Please hurry,' he kept saying. 'It is most important that I get back to my pit.'

But the marshal was inclined to take his own time.

Chapter 8

The Speed Six Fights for Her Life

THE dawn mist was worse than ever this year. It was a matter of feeling your way around, anticipating the corners by the characteristics of the road verge and relying on your memory of every slight curve and gradient of the course.

Johnny had folded *Diane*'s windscreen flat and had raised himself higher on the seat to increase visibility. His lap speed had dropped, but all the cars had reduced speed – it would have been suicide to do otherwise – and he was actually getting round five miles an hour faster than the two leading Atlantics.

The smallest cars were the greatest danger. Not all of them hugged the right bank as they should have done, and suddenly out of the grey shadows twin red tail-lights, like the menacing eyes of an animal, would race towards the Bentley's radiator, and Johnny would jerk the wheel to the left and squeeze by as best he could, often with his inside wheels on the grass verge.

He caught Number 10 Atlantic under the Dunlop bridge four laps after Blackie's warning signals. He had passed it half a dozen times since that first terrific dice before the pit-stop in the late afternoon, and it was clear that this third car of the team just did not have the power of the other two.

Johnny swung out to pass, expecting no difficulty and no danger. Blackie's message had clearly indicated that if there was trouble it would come from Barnaby James himself.

The white dotted line down the centre of the track was an invaluable guide in this fog, and the Atlantic was well over to the right of it when Johnny started to go by. But to his horror the little dark shape swerved suddenly across the line into the full glare of Johnny's yellow fog-lamp less than ten feet ahead of him.

He stamped on his brakes hard, the Bentley's tail reacting with a violent wag that nearly threw the car out of control. 'What's the madman up to?' he shouted, and flicked his fog-lamp on and off in protest. 'Get over to the right – get over and let me by.'

At the top of the rise, with the Atlantic still barring his way, Johnny tried, against all regulations, to pass him on the right. But again the car swung over just before he came up level with it, and Johnny fell back, fuming with rage.

Jon Jeans had increased speed, too. After the two sudden brake applications, Johnny had no chance to draw level before the Esses, and on the straight before Tertre Rouge he lost the Atlantic momentarily in the fog.

The illuminated '10' loomed up before him again in the swirling grey half-light. The Atlantic was going much faster than it had been the last time Johnny had passed it, almost as if it was tempting Johnny on, challenging him to try again to get by. And he knew he had to pass. He could not afford to be baulked while the other two Atlantics increased their lead.

'S O S Mulsanne.' That had been Blackie's signal. How he had got wind of this threat did not matter for the moment. What mattered was that Barnaby James' henchman had planned to hold him up, and, if pressed, to risk a shunt to stall off the threat of the Bentley. . . .

Both cars were racing blindly down the straight at

over 130 m.p.h., the Bentley gaining only a yard at a time on the smaller car. Imperceptibly Johnny edged *Diane* over to the left, brought the high nose up level with the low tail of the Atlantic. His front wheel hubs were running alongside the rear wheel hubs of the little car. Then, just when he thought he was safely past, he saw the low, hunched figure in the other driver's seat turn the wheel sharply to the left.

Only by throwing all his weight on to the brake pedal did Johnny avoid a collision this time. The Bentley swung broadside along the road, Johnny fighting with the wheel to regain control. His speed had dropped to under three figures when at last he had *Diane* centred on the white line again, and the Atlantic had disappeared into the mist.

Johnny had never been so angry in his life. Muttering invectives under his breath, he put his right foot hard on the accelerator pedal.

It must have been less than a mile from the end of the straight that he caught up with the Atlantic again. It had slowed up and was swinging regularly from side to side of the track. Johnny decided that it was time for a bold policy. It was surely as important for Jon Jeans to avoid a collision as it was to prevent the Bentley getting past, and if it was to run into a heavyweight contest, *Diane* had twice the weight and twice the height as advantages.

The mad duel continued for another few seconds, both cars rocking in rhythm from one verge of the road to the other while Johnny awaited the right moment to make his attack.

At 100 m.p.h. things happen at a speed that cannot be conceived by the ordinary motorist. It is usually impossible for witnesses to reconstruct a crisis in detail on a racing circuit; and on the Mulsanne straight, with the first rays of the early morning sun beginning to break up the mist, there were no witnesses at that Le Mans dawn to see what followed.

Johnny brought the Bentley right alongside the Atlantic by a superb piece of timing. He caught a fleeting glimpse of Jon Jeans' white face beneath the visor glancing across at the big green car. Then the Atlantic closed in. Three yards, two yards, two feet separated the flying machines. Contact now would mean disaster, and the Bentley's left wheels were already brushing the verge.

The Atlantic was matching *Diane*'s speed and the gap narrowed to a few inches. 'A touch more – give out that little extra,' Johnny begged the Bentley – and she answered nobly, drawing ahead a little so that she was almost free from the closing trap, with Johnny using all the strength in his arms against the wheel shudder.

Perhaps Jon Jeans' courage had already failed him, and the last flick of the Atlantic's front wheels was beyond his control. Perhaps it was a last gesture of bravery, or fear of Barnaby James if he failed. No one else will ever know. But as the Bentley's rear wheels slipped out of the deadly gap, the Atlantic's left front hub just touched the bare tyre of the other machine.

It was nothing more than a light tap, but it was enough. Johnny felt *Diane*'s tail slide out on to the grass. He flicked the steering-wheel into the skid and the Bentley's tail instantly reversed its direction, thrusting hard against the Atlantic's body.

Jon Jeans' car was quickly disposed of. It shot like a bolt across the width of the road, rose up over the verge in a cloud of sand and earth, somersaulted on to its back, and ploughed a deep, straight furrow across a field. Two minutes later the front wheels were still spinning in the air like the nervous twitching of a dead animal when Jon Jeans dragged himself out of the wreckage with a fractured skull, a broken right arm, and three cracked ribs.

Diane stayed on the road almost to Mulsanne corner. Her sheer weight was an asset. But more important were the skilled hands at the wheel and the determination of the driver that guided them.

Two complete circles she made, with Johnny letting her have her head all the way, and his long experience helping him to resist the temptation to stab at the brakes, for that would have finished the battle before it had begun. She came out of the last 360 degrees pointing forward, and Johnny corrected, without trouble, the new spin that began to develop. But *Diane* was still not stable, her tail twitching like a misused thoroughbred; and it was one of the sharp swings that by an unhappy chance sent the Bentley's left rear wheel slamming against a kilometre stone at the roadside.

This was too much for the old car. The tyre threw its tread, the wheel buckled, and then instantly shattered into a thousand pieces of steel. *Diane*, down into the sixties now, slewed across the road half on her rear axle, spun twice more out of Johnny's control, rose up over the verge, and slammed into the ditch.

The speed had dropped from 40 m.p.h. to zero in a few seconds. For the driver, this could lead to only one result. Johnny was shot forward from his seat, the steering-wheel thrust against his chest, and his head rammed the dash. . . .

The whirling, spinning hectic world closed about Johnny like a black curtain. He felt a sharp, agonizing jar; the clearing dawn mist thickened to a dense fog; the confused sounds of engine and exhaust blended in with the terrifying shriek of ripping tyres, were shut off with merciful suddenness.

The champion, for once, had been defeated. Johnny Wild sprawled, helpless and concussed, across the Bentley's cockpit, while the cars shot past ten feet away. *La Ronde Impitoyable* was continuing its merciless pace. . . .

Three precious minutes passed before the telephone rang in the Bentley pit. Mervyn, sick with anxiety at *Diane*'s disappearance, grabbed it up.

'Well . . . well. What is it, man?' A stream of incomprehensible sounds came through the earpiece. 'Speak in English, can't you? Don't understand a word.' His face was creased with irritation. 'Now more slowly. Yes, near Mulsanne. The Bentley is finished,' he repeated. 'What do you mean "finished"? How badly damaged?'

Mervyn nodded his head several times as he listened to the slowly spoken sentences in broken English, while the two young apprentices stood on each side, mouths open in wondering horror.

'And the driver? Insensible, you say? Out, but not too badly hurt, eh? All right, all right. Now don't you let anyone touch that car. No – one – is – to – touch – it,' he repeated slowly. 'All right? Good.'

He slammed the receiver down on its cradle and spun around on Bert and Harry. It was not in Mervyn's nature to waste time on curses and regrets. Swift, precise action was called for. During wartime in Britain a notice had hung on the walls of many pubs and restaurants: 'We are not interested in the possibilities of defeat,' he had read. 'They do not exist.' This bold maxim Mervyn applied to motor-racing, and it had led to many unexpected victories.

'Harry, get me a bicycle,' he ordered. 'I don't care

how or where, but bring it to this door within a minute. Bert, hand me the other torch. You stay here, do you understand, and when Mr Black gets back, tell him what's happened. Tell him I've gone over to the car and that I'm going to get it back into working order. If Mr Wild's still unconscious, he'll have to come over to Mulsanne and drive it back to the pit. There'll be a message waiting for him at the marshal's box at Mulsanne corner. He can call them up on the telephone.

'Have everything ready for a pit-stop,' he called from the door. 'Everything: new tyres, oil, plenty of water – the lot. And, most important of all, guard this place with your life. Put the ·38 in your pocket. Those Atlantic boys seem to have gone mad and may be up to anything if they're ready to try to murder a driver....'

The resourceful, red-headed Harry had begged a bicycle from a gendarme, and he was holding it out ready for Mervyn to leap on to the saddle when he came out of the back door of the pit.

Mervyn threw himself on it like an Olympian athlete. But before he pedalled off, he glanced up at the great long scoreboard, illuminated high above them. There were new red diagonal eliminating lines across two more cars; one was Number 10 Atlantic, and the other Number 1 Bentley.

Mervyn leaped to the ground again on a wave of furious indignation. He cupped his mouth in his hands and bawled up at the bewildering mass of illuminated figures and names. 'You're wrong, you fools,' he shouted. 'Take that red mark off the Bentley. It hasn't retired.' But he might as well have given his orders to a Piccadilly Circus advertisement at night. 'What's more, it's still going to win,' he added, 'so brush up your electronics, you crazy machine.'

Then the little Welshman was away, pedalling furiously off between the service trucks, through the enclosure gate, along a farm-track, across a field of growing corn, over half a dozen ditches, and then down a short length of road leading to Mulsanne. It was more than four miles, and he made it in less than fifteen minutes.

The mist had cleared right away and the sun was touching the topmost branches of the pines when the wooden hut, with its wireless aerial and string of telephone wires, came into sight. 'It'd have taken me half an hour round by road,' thought Mervyn with satisfaction. 'Only goes to show two wheels are better than four.'

Number 8 Atlantic screamed round the near-hairpin on a perfect line as Mervyn threw down the bicycle and ran into the hut. A B.R.C. and a Pegoso followed, drowning his voice.

But Mervyn did not have to repeat his question to the officials in the hut. A hundred yards up the road a little group, as transfixed as all men who stare at disaster, stood about the crashed Bentley. This was what he had expected, of course; it was what he had come for. But the sudden sight of his beloved *Diane* sprawled across the ditch like some wounded old elephant, gave him a sudden stab of pain to his heart.

As he ran nearer he saw that one of the headlamps was smashed and half twisted off its bracket, that the right front mudguard was twisted sideways, and that, while the front of the car with one wheel in the shallow ditch was at an angle, the rear appeared to be level. The voice on the phone had said something about a smashed wheel. 'It must be the left rear wheel that's gone,' thought Mervyn. 'Hope to heaven the axle's taken the strain and the frame isn't fractured.'

He broke through the little crowd and darted around

the car, casting quick, expert glances at the damage. The chassis was all right, thanks to the massive construction. No space frame, tubular alloy modern box of tricks could have stood the terrific shock, Mervyn reckoned. It would have folded up like a concertina. The only worry was the delicate disc-brake mechanism. No amount of automatic compensation would make *Diane* driveable at speed with three brakes. . . .

And what of Johnny? If Blackie did not turn up in time, would Johnny have revived enough to take the wheel again if Mervyn tackled the repairs?

A white ambulance had drawn up a dozen yards away, and two white-coated figures were among the little group around Johnny's outstretched figure on the ground. Mervyn ran over and knelt down beside him.

Johnny was lying on a stretcher under a pile of blankets, his head propped up on a pillow. His face was dead white and there was a great blue weal in the centre of his forehead, and a gash across his cheek, which one of the ambulance men was dressing with a square of lint. His eyes were closed, he was breathing normally, and he looked, Mervyn thought, quite at peace with the world.

'How long will it be before he comes round?' he asked one of the attendants, who shrugged his shoulders in uncertainty. 'Looks all right to me. Can't we chuck a bucket of water over him?'

The attendant stared at him in horror. 'What are you saying?'

'Why not?' Mervyn broke in. 'It's what they do to boxers, isn't it?' He was never very sympathetic to personal injury in others – though he was the most fussy patient himself – and he knew that a violent return to consciousness, and to the wheel of *Diane*, was what Johnny would most have wanted.

'We are afraid for his ribs,' said the attendant in halting English. 'We must X-ray him at the hospital. It will not be possible for him to motor any more.' And they began lifting the stretcher off the ground to slide it into the ambulance.

'Bah!' said Mervyn angrily, knowing that it would be useless to argue any further. 'Nothing much wrong with him. He'll biff you one when he comes round, man, that he will. And he'll throw your wretched X-ray machine out of the window when he realizes you've lost him the race.'

'Lay off it, chum,' chimed in one of the English spectators. 'Blimey, you won't get that old hulk back on the road again.'

Mervyn pushed his way past them, waving his arms in all directions. The storm of anger broke into a hurricane. 'You're all mad. Every one of you. The Bentley's not only getting back into the race. . . . It's going to win – DO YOU HEAR!' he shouted to the whole group of listless, overcoated figures.

Sleeves rolled up, the tool-roll and the jack on the ground beside him, Mervyn set to like a whirlwind. This was a situation where the Le Mans regulations were a help, for they specified not only that a spare wheel must be carried, but that all tools used for repairs and maintenance must be stowed in the car.

Up with the rear axle, off with the spare wheel at the rear, knock off the hub holding on the last fragments of the old shattered wheel. There was a dent in the cooling ejector and the water from the cooling system was draining away through a leak in the pipe. Back axle was O.K., though. Straight as the day it left the foundry. . . . *Diane* would be all right.

The only worry was the driver. Where in blazes was

Blackie? Mervyn had left a message at the hut that Blackie must come over at double speed when he got back. But there was no sign of him.

A strip of adhesive linen tape fixed the water leak. 'Push the brake pedal, please,' he asked the official who was watching his every move like a hawk for any infringement. But the official shook his head. 'No assistance must be given,' he told him firmly. 'That would mean instant disqualification.'

Mervyn grunted and ran around the car to do the job himself. 'We'll get you back on the road, me dear,' he murmured, patting *Diane*'s bonnet. 'Never fear. Blackie'll be here in a minute.'

He'd better be, Mervyn thought to himself. They had lost fifteen minutes already, but the repairs were nearly complete. He lifted the great, heavy spare wheel and slipped it on to the stub axle. The knock-on hub followed, and this he locked firmly with the soft-headed brass hammer. With the same hammer he beat the front mudguard roughly back into shape and knocked out the fragments of glass from the headlamp.

A bigger crowd had gathered now. They stood in silence, watching apparently without either interest or amusement Mervyn's lightning movements around the car.

He leaped into the driver's seat, switched on the ignition, glanced around the instruments, put the gear into neutral, and pressed the starter button.

The result brought some life into the group of spectators. They leaped back as if a bomb had gone off when *Diane* started up, and Mervyn revved the 6½-litre engine to 3,500 r.p.m. 'Couldn't be healthier,' he considered. 'If Blackie can get her out of this ditch then all's well.'

But where was the fellow? Mervyn switched off and

stood up in the seat in an effort to catch sight of him through the trees. There was still no sign of him; and the ambulance bearing the unconscious Johnny had driven away. Here was the Bentley, a sound car, still in a strong position, but with no driver. It was enough to send anyone to the point of exasperation, and even Mervyn's control broke down. He fumed and raged, beat his fists on the back of the seat, and called out furiously and uselessly, 'Blackie, where are you, you fool? Blackie, BLACKIE!'

And now the crowd sniggered and smiled and nudged each other in amused delight at this wild Welshman in the ancient racing-car.

Mervyn's sanity was restored by the arrival at that moment of two cars. One was Number 8 Atlantic, with Barnaby James back at the wheel, tearing down the straight towards the corner, well in the lead and sounding as healthy as it had at the start.

The other car came silently and with infinite dignity down the farm-track which led, on the inside of the circuit, to the grandstands. Sitting high up in the driver's seat, in tweed overcoat over his breeches, and deerstalker hat, was the Duke of Bucks. The Silver Ghost Rolls-Royce drew up gently alongside the stranded Bentley, and the Duke unhurriedly opened the door and climbed down. He took in the situation at a glance and grimaced sadly at Mervyn. 'There, but for the grace of Barnaby James,' he said, pointing to Number 8 Atlantic streaking out of the corner, 'goes the car that ought by now to be running a poor second.'

'You've guessed right, sir,' growled Mervyn.

'Up to his tricks – and no way of proving it, eh? I thought so the moment they flashed the two retirements on the board.'

'*Diane* hasn't retired,' said Mervyn indignantly. 'Lacking a driver, that's all. Where is that ass, Blackie? Have you seen him, sir?'

'What's the matter with you? Should think they'd stretch the regulations and let you take her back to the pit. Seems to me it's that – or admitting defeat.' He suddenly smiled knowingly at the engineer, and, as if he had just remembered the fact, added, 'But of course you're not much of a hand with a steering-wheel, eh?'

Mervyn stared angrily at the Duke, and gave a little involuntary shudder. Then in a sudden, frightening wave the truth of the dilemma swept over him. Somebody, somehow, had to get *Diane* back to the pit. If anyone else drove her she would be disqualified instantly. If she remained here, helpless in the ditch, all the taunts and wisecracks would be justified, and all the prophecies of the smart journalists would be realized.

And Barnaby James? Barnaby James, who had added injuries to insults and foul play to injuries, would go on to win the dirtiest motor-race since the sport had begun more than half a century ago. . . .

The Duke of Bucks watched anxiously, and with some amusement, the changing emotions reflected in Mervyn's face – puzzlement, bewilderment, nervousness, horror, and finally grim resolution.

With the great decision finally made, Mervyn characteristically acted on it with speed. 'As a matter of fact, I'm a very good driver,' he told the Duke solemnly.

Mervyn had sat in *Diane*'s driver's seat hundreds of times. He knew the position, and the feel of all the controls, and he understood the mechanics of driving – of the cause and effect of the operation – better than Johnny or Blackie. But the practice of driving was a closed book, and it was hardly fair that on this, his first trial drive, he

117

should be faced with the terrifying problem of getting a two-ton, 6½-litre monster out of a shallow ditch and on to a racing circuit that was alive with flying cars.

But none of this weighed with Mervyn. All that mattered now was that the Bentley was going back to the pit, and he was going to conduct it there.

He started the engine again and engaged first gear. You lifted the foot slowly from the clutch pedal, he had been told – and the Duke, standing alongside, confirmed this. 'Easy does it,' he told him above the roar of the rising revs. 'Get her moving forward with plenty of power on before you pull over the wheel and get her out of the ditch.'

'All right, all right,' Mervyn said irritably. 'I know. Let me alone,' as if he could manage quite well without advice. He looked like a little pinched gnome, almost swallowed up in the Bentley's driver's seat, and it did not seem possible that he could even see over the top of the folded windshield.

The Bentley moved forward a yard with a convulsive jerk – and stalled with the engine dead. He tried again, and this time Mervyn made a dozen yards, sending up clods of earth and stones from the back wheelspin. He pressed hard on the accelerator, almost disappearing under the dash in doing so, and heaved the wheel over to the left.

To his astonishment – and to the small cheer from the crowd – *Diane* lifted herself bodily out of the ditch and came down on an even keel on the road verge.

Easier than I thought, Mervyn told himself with satisfaction. Not frightening at all really. As he drove on to the road, he did not see the Duke of Bucks' wave of congratulation, and then the frantic whirling of his arms as he glanced up the track. Nor did he hear the shouts of warning from everyone in sight. He felt suddenly happy and full of confidence. Driving was fun. Driving was easy.

And, of course, you drove on the left. He always bicycled on the left-hand side of the road.

The blue 2-litre French Aerial was travelling very fast indeed. There was only one other car ahead of it in its class, and it was only half a lap in the lead. The driver intended to catch that car – or blow up his engine in the attempt. A mile back the corner had been clear, and the Frenchman had left the braking to the very last moment. But he had not reckoned on the intervention of a huge green vehicle, quite as big, it seemed, as an army truck, which slowly and deliberately crossed the road in front of him, like a soporific cow returning from the milking-sheds.

Mervyn not only had the engine revs screaming as he slipped the clutch, but he was much too pleased with himself to hear the rubber whine of locked tyres biting into the road surface and rising to a crescendo as the car slewed helplessly towards him.

By some incredible stroke of good fortune he remembered that, of course, he was not in England now, and that in France, for some odd reason, they drove on the right. So he slowly but firmly swung the wheel over, and aimed the car at Mulsanne corner on the right-hand side of the road.

Snaking like a tadpole, and with her driver fighting furiously, the Aerial slipped by with six inches to spare.

Imperturbable, delighted with life and with this new sensation he had only just discovered, Mervyn took *Diane* round Mulsanne corner behind the shaken Aerial and at a quarter of her speed. Why had he never tried this before? Wonderful experience, he thought. And he pressed down harder on the accelerator. Twice he tried changing gear, the cogs protesting with a terrible crashing sound; then at last he got into second, but only at the price of sliding right off the seat and under the steering-wheel.

It was zigzag, wander and twist all the way along to the next corner, the other drivers passing with their hearts in their mouths. After the corner, Mervyn managed to get into top. And then there was no holding him. Speed got a grip on the little Welshman. He did not see it, because he dared not look down, but there was more than a hundred on the clock before he thought he had better ease off a little for Arnage.

The sharp right-hander he took at a speed rather above what Johnny would have considered the limit, and he did not bother to change down. Changing gear was a bore, Mervyn had decided.

At White House he put all his weight on to the accelerator. He shouted out with delight at this new surge of power, and slipped by, without quite knowing what he was doing, a B.R.C., which had to swerve suddenly as the Bentley cut in just in front.

'I've passed a car!' he suddenly realized. 'Nothing to it. I'll pass the lot of them. Look out, here I come!'

Up towards the grandstands, weaving with a slight drunken lurch from side to side of the road, came *Diane* – a new driver at the helm, and an unprecedented speed on the speedometer. . . .

'He's all right, then,' shouted Blackie in delight, racing across to the counter and staring down the track. Everyone had heard the old familiar thunder of *Diane*'s exhaust note which had been silent for more than half an hour.

'Good old Johnny. Trust him not to care about a dirty shunt.' Blackie had just arrived back at the pit after his questioning and eventual release by the gendarmes. His fury had been overwhelmed by his anxiety about *Diane* and Johnny, for he had heard the commentator's announcement of the crash and retirement.

Worry had changed to excited delight within a few seconds, and then again to surprise as he saw the strange course the Bentley was steering, as he saw her wheels lock when the brakes were applied with terrific force, and she came to a rocking standstill fifty yards beyond her pit in the dead centre of the track.

'That's not Johnny,' Blackie exclaimed to the apprentices. 'By golly; it's – No, it can't be. But it is ... it's Mervyn. Hey, what are you up to?' he shouted.

A dozen officials were wondering the same thing and were storming around him like a swarm of angry bees, waving their flags and their arms frantically.

When Blackie arrived, Mervyn just looked up at him with an idiotic grin. The engine had stalled, and the other machines were racing past a few yards away at undiminished speed.

'Get out, you madman!' Blackie yelled, and half-dragged the dazed Welshman from the driver's seat. Blackie took his place in a flash and cautiously backed the battered-looking Bentley to her pit counter.

Chapter 9

. . . And the Chequered Flag Falls

A RED fire extinguisher was the first thing Johnny saw when he opened his eyes. It was held to the wall by a metal clip. Then his eyes swung to a box on a shelf with a big red cross on the side, a window of darkened glass, and walls of gleaming white paint.

Of course, he remembered, he had been fighting for *Diane*, fighting for her life as well as his own. She had slewed one way and then the other, from side to side, while he had countered with violent swings on the wheel. . . . And it had not been *Diane*'s fault. The old girl had not let him down. One of the Atlantics had deliberately baulked and then rammed him. Jon Jeans' Atlantic, no doubt under the orders of Barnaby James.

The memory of that mad battle along Mulsanne was screened in Johnny's consciousness like a speeded-up movie film; and with it came a growing anger; and with the anger realization of his present position.

He was not in a hospital ward, for the little white room was swaying and rocking about. He was obviously in an ambulance, and an ambulance that was in a hurry, judging by the way the driver was taking the corners. But he had no business to be wrapped up in blankets on an ambulance stretcher. Le Mans was at its most critical stage, and he must get back to his car.

But when Johnny sat up and swung his legs off the stretcher, a pair of hands firmly pressed him back again. A male nurse smiled down at him. '*Doucement, doucement, restez, monsieur, restez,*' he said gently.

'*Restez*, my foot!' exclaimed Johnny. 'I've got to get back to the track. Just stop this nonsense, and stop this ambulance There's nothing wrong with me.' He jerked himself to his feet, feeling rather giddy, but fighting fit, and pushed aside the protesting nurse.

Johnny's fists crashed against the ambulance's panelling, and he glowered angrily through the window into the cab at the backs of the driver and the second nurse. 'Stop this thing!' he shouted. 'You're making a mistake, there's nothing wrong with me.'

The first nurse, certain that this was a case of shock hysteria, dragged with all his might at Johnny's shoulders. He was finished with pleading and was cursing angrily in French. But Johnny disregarded him, beyond shrugging him off as if he were an annoying insect, and before the ambulance had shrieked to a halt, had opened the double doors at the rear.

The other two men put up a brief fight. Whether they surrendered so quickly because Johnny seemed too formidable a foe, or because they suddenly realized that he must be in his right mind after all, Johnny never knew. The driver picked himself out of the ditch, the second nurse arose slowly from his sitting position in the middle of the road, and they bundled themselves into the driving cab to Johnny's order in silence.

'Now where in blazes are we?' asked Johnny as he put the ambulance into reverse and backed it into a farm entrance. 'Half-way to the town, eh? You're a trio of chumps, aren't you? How do you think Blackie can get on without a relief driver?'

Soon 75 kilometres per hour was on the speedometer, and the road was a rough one; never before had the Frenchmen been driven like this. They exchanged nervous glances, and the driver spoke hesitantly to Johnny between rapid bounces up and down. 'But your car, monsieur. She ees no goot. *Fini.*'

'*Diane* finished?' laughed Johnny. 'Don't be silly. I'll bet she's as right as rain. You don't know what a beating that car can take. If I'm only bruised, she'll hardly be touched.'

His two passengers clutched at one another as Johnny put the heavy ambulance around a blind corner flat out. Ahead of him he could see the flags floating gaily in the early-morning sun above the grandstands, and the noise of racing engines rising to top revs broke through the sound of the ambulance's motor. The race was still on. It was like returning to a brilliant, exciting party from which one had had to break away. . . .

'But, *monsieur*,' said the nurse, 'it was very bad – that concussion, it was bad. And your reebs, *monsieur*,' he went on, reaching for the dash as Johnny rammed on the brakes. 'They – may – be – broken.'

'Oh, nuts!' exclaimed Johnny impatiently, and in a resounding English accent ordered, '*Sonnez la cloche*, can't you?'

There were people all over the road and they were not getting out of the way fast enough. The clanging bell did the trick, however, and they scattered like ants before the flying ambulance.

Under the Tertre Rouge tunnel they shot, along the rough track, past the car park, and into the reserved enclosure behind the pits. One or two startled mechanics saw the wild-looking figure leap from the ambulance driver's seat; he was in torn, oily overalls with streaks of blood down the front; there was a heavy bandage across his cheek, and his long, black hair was floating all over the place.

'Thanks for the aid and ministrations,' he shouted

over his shoulder. 'Sorry I had to be rather firm.' He threw open the door marked BENTLEY, and demanded loudly of the three startled faces, 'Where's *Diane*?'

That the green Bentley had not been disqualified was entirely due to Mervyn's impassioned persuasion of the officials, although of course it was his own unauthorized drive around from Mulsanne that had led to the threat.

The regulations were quite clear on the point: Only the named qualified drivers could take the wheel of machines during the race.

'But I said to them, man, this is what I said,' explained Mervyn to Johnny. 'If you arrest one of our drivers and the other one is shunted off the road by a piece of dirty driving, then whose fault is it? They didn't like the bit about "dirty driving" and told me I had no grounds for such an accusation. I didn't tell them we had plenty of grounds. I thought it better to leave that alone for now.'

'Did they catch Blackie actually signalling?' Johnny asked.

'Luckily not. He'd finished and was getting back into the cover of the woods. Of course it was against all regulations for anyone – even one of the drivers – to be there. But Blackie spun some tale about watching the behaviour of the car as it came out of the corner. And after filling in a lot of stupid forms he was at last released by the authority of the prefect of the gendarmerie.'

Johnny warmed his hands on the mug of tea brewed by Harry. He heard the deep boom of the Bentley coming up the rise and watched with a feeling of pride as she rushed by under Blackie's guidance. Johnny lifted the mug in the gesture of a toast, and he caught a glimpse of Blackie's raised thumb of acknowledgement before he changed to third for the Dunlop bridge bend.

'Ah, that'll cheer him on,' said Mervyn. 'He thought he'd be coping single-handed.'

'He's doing all right,' said Johnny. 'No need for him to worry.'

The red diagonal line had been removed from the Bentley's name on the scoreboard. She was back in fifth position, behind the two Atlantics by six laps, and on the same lap and rapidly catching up again a Pegoso and the 2-litre French Aerial. *Diane* might be looking rather forlorn with her battered bodywork, but she was sounding as sweet and healthy as ever.

Johnny stretched and yawned. 'First time I've slept during Le Mans,' he said. 'And I suppose I couldn't do much about it. Never mind – a spell at the wheel'll wake me up.' He glanced at Mervyn's face. He was back at his precise timekeeping again. And yet, thought Johnny, a subtle change had seemed to come over him, a perceptible straightening of those shoulders which had seemed always bowed in defiance of a hostile world, an easing of those deep lines of petulance and worry on his face.

'Tell me about your little dice round from Mulsanne,' Johnny asked him.

Mervyn looked up from his charts. Johnny realized it was not his imagination. There *was* a new sparkle in those eyes, a new expression of tolerance about his mouth. Just as though, thought Johnny to himself, the Welshman had had an 'experience'.

'Yes,' said Mervyn thoughtfully and slowly. 'Yes – that was quite exciting, man.'

Eight a.m. Eight hours to go. The local papers had printed special Sunday-morning editions, with thick headlines about the race and more photographs of the cars, but in action this time, on the corners and along the straights. There were several pictures of *Diane*, and one or two articles, written before the crash, expressing surprise at the performance she was putting up, though none of the writers believed she would stay the course.

'Positions at midnight,' was boxed on the front page of all the papers. *Diane* had been lying sixth then, but now all except two of the cars ahead of her had retired or crashed. For Blackie had brought her back to third place, well ahead now of the comparatively slow Pegoso and the 2-litre Aerial.

And yet the Bentley's position was not a happy one, though neither Johnny nor Mervyn had expressed anxiety. Eight hours to go and nearly six laps to make up. Over fifty miles to gain in the last third of the race, and it was certain that the two Atlantics, with their commanding lead, would not be stretching themselves to the limit at present.

At last Mervyn broke the worried silence. 'How are you feeling, man? You had a good old knocking about, you know.'

'Never been better,' Johnny told him. A huge hot breakfast of bacon and three eggs had cleared away the last of his dizziness and slight sense of being detached from the world. 'Why?' he asked Mervyn curiously. 'You're not going to start mollycoddling me like those misguided ambulance men, are you? All I want to do is to get back into *Diane*.'

Mervyn smiled up at Johnny, and made him realize that he had never before seen him look actually mischievous. 'I wasn't doubting that you could drive, Johnny man,' he laughed. 'I was going to ask if you could take her right through to the finish.'

Johnny did not doubt for one second that he could.

There was no suggestion of uncertainty in his voice as he answered at once, 'Of course I can. Good idea.'

Johnny was too modest to add what, in fact, was the truth: that it was their only hope of wresting the laurels of victory from Barnaby James. A good, sound driver could hold his position in the race to the end, just as Blackie was holding it – and even gaining a few seconds on every lap. But something more than that was needed, the something extra – the extra touch of dash and verve, that last touch of courage which is beyond the borders of mere bravery, that ability to drive a little faster through every corner and to coax from a piece of machinery the ultimate maximum of its power output.

Only Johnny could do that, and he would have to do it to the very limit if he was to make up those fifty miles. They would not be able to afford to hand *Diane* back to Blackie for the second of the three remaining spells of the race. Johnny, in fact, would have to drive right through on his own. . . .

It was like the opening laps all over again. At midday the last of the crowds had left the stalls and stands, the booths and dodge-'em cars, the cafés in the marquees, and had packed in behind the twenty rows of spectators against the barriers. This, surely, everyone was saying, is *the* Le Mans – the greatest of them all.

After a period of quiet in the early morning, when it seemed that nothing but the worst misfortune could prevent the Atlantics from running away with the race, the tempo and the excitement had increased.

The one difference from the previous afternoon was the weather; almost by tradition now, Le Mans was wet for the last few hours, and shortly before midday the dark clouds had rolled up, and the heavens had opened in a great downpour. But none of the spectators took any notice of the pouring rain. The Bentley–Atlantic duel was far too exciting for that.

To Johnny the rain had been a godsend for which he had been hoping since he had taken over from Blackie amid cheers from the grandstand at half-past eight. Modest as he was, Johnny knew he was a good driver in the dry; in the wet, he knew he was unsurpassed, and he had been taking full advantage of the fact.

Everyone on the circuit with a watch – stop-watch, wrist-watch or pocket-watch – was timing the closing gap between Number 1 Bentley and Number 9 Atlantic, with Johnny's old friend at the wheel. Mike Corrigan, true to his word and his loyalty to his firm, was battling furiously to keep the Bentley off his tail. He knew well enough that he was the last obstacle Johnny faced before tackling Barnaby James himself, half a lap ahead and going great guns.

By one o'clock Johnny had got within ten seconds of the Irishman, the two cars screaming around, their tyres ripping through sheets of water on the sodden track and sending great clouds of spray high into the air. Accelerating away from the corners under full throttle, their rear wheels whipped from side to side like the tails of angry snakes; a touch of brake on this wet surface, and the driver was at once correcting a dangerous skid.

Johnny caught Mike at last on Mulsanne, creeping up foot by foot as they went past the Hippodrome café. Five times before since he had taken over he had got past Mike in order to make up those lost laps; the last three times had been in the rain, too. But this time, as they both knew, Johnny was actually displacing the Atlantic from number two position – the Bentley was second in the race.

The 'All Out' signs had long been taken in from both the Atlantic and Bentley pits. Everyone at Le Mans, from the youngest child to the drivers themselves, knew that it was full-throttle driving to the end of the race.

The little contests taking place among the other surviving cars for the Index of Performance handicap prize and the class wins were unnoticed. There might have been only three machines on the Sarthe circuit that wet Sunday afternoon: a majestic old Bentley sandwiched and battling for its life between two Atlantics.

'Well, this is it. Here she comes,' said Mervyn, catching a glimpse of Johnny beating up from White House through the downpour.

It was the final pit-stop. Everything might depend on the speed at which they could refuel and top up *Diane* and change her wheels.

They had once done it in one minute twenty seconds in practice. They must beat that record now.

They were all ready; the two apprentices with the oil, water, hydraulic fluid, the petrol hose swung out; Mervyn standing with the waiting *plombeur*; Blackie with a glass of hot orange juice, a warm, wet towel to wipe down Johnny, and a clean dry one. Behind them and out of their way was the Duke of Bucks, hopping first on one foot and then on the other, longing to lend a hand.

In the stands everyone was on their feet, silent and tense with excitement.

Johnny was out of the car before it had stopped, staggering slightly after the long hours in the seat. His bandage had long since been torn off by the wind, and the ugly red line on his cheek, the blue weal on his forehead when he dragged off his helmet, and the haggard, drawn expression on his face – as though he had reached the limit – made an agonizing sight.

Harry had the quick-lift jack under the front axle, but Johnny turned on him and pulled it out of his hand. 'Leave 'em alone,' he shouted hoarsely. 'Get on with the refuelling, they'll last.'

Mervyn dashed up to him, and Blackie leaped down from the counter and clutched his arm. 'What do you mean?' they demanded together. 'You can't run on those tyres any longer.'

'Leave 'em alone,' he repeated, turning on his friends angrily. 'We'll save a few seconds if we leave those wheels on. I'm driving, aren't I? Do as I say or I quit. D'you hear me!' he shouted, frantic with rage. 'You're wasting seconds.'

It was no use arguing with Johnny while he was in this state, and there was no doubt he would carry out his threat. It was near-suicide, for there was hardly any tread left on the racing tyres – but what could you do? Mervyn tossed aside the jack and tackled the engine while Harry finished off the refuelling.

Blackie half-carried Johnny to the counter and propped him up against it like a tailor's dummy. No use recriminating, no use warning, he reckoned. Encouragement and confidence, they're what he wants. Blackie tipped the glass of orange juice to his mouth. 'You'll get him,' he told him firmly. 'Can't fail, Johnny. You're gaining like mad. This is your race, Johnny boy.'

He threw aside the glass and wiped Johnny's terrible face gently with the warm towel 'Never seen you drive like this before. By golly, this is the race of your life, Johnny – and you're going to get that low snake. Do you hear, Johnny?' Blackie said gently. 'You're going to get him.'

Blackie took the dry towel away from Johnny's face, leaving it grey with fatigue but clean again. And now there was the beginning of a grin about his mouth – a suggestion of the old light-hearted Johnny. 'Sure I'm going to get him,' he said.

Mervyn's voice called out urgently, 'O.K. Off you go.' Bert was tightening the last of the leather bonnet-straps. *Diane* was ready for the last round.

Refreshed, and with Blackie's words of encouragement still ringing in his ears, Johnny dropped into the driver's seat. Back in the arena again, the slow hesitancy of his movements was forgotten. His hand flashed for the starter-button. *Diane* burst into life and was away as a thousand stop-watches clicked. One minute five seconds – that was all it had taken. It was a prodigious speed for a pit-stop. And Barnaby James, ten minutes before, had taken two minutes twenty-five. So Johnny's decision to drive on with the old tyres had gained him two and a half miles, or nearly a third of a lap.

Blackie fell into a seat beside the Duke. 'Phew!' he sighed. 'The man's mad. Those tyres won't last an hour.'

The old Duke looked seriously at him. 'Yes, he may be mad,' he said slowly, 'and he also may be very brave – he may have known it was the only thing to do. . . .'

It was not until after three o'clock, with less than an hour of the race to run, that Johnny caught sight of the distant cloud of spray which could only have been Barnaby James' Atlantic turning off Mulsanne. There was no means of identifying the car, but he knew it bore the Number 8 from Mervyn's signals, which had kept him informed of the slowly narrowing gap.

The number '20' had hung out from the pit the last time he had passed; the lap before it had been twenty-three seconds; and before that twenty-four seconds.

'Twenty seconds,' thought Johnny, 'at 120 m.p.h.' – and they were not lapping at much less than that in spite of the rain – 'was two-thirds of a mile. About twelve hundred yards. If I can't make up twelve hundred yards before four o'clock, I'll retire from racing.'

But the challenge was not so simple as that. Motor-racing is rarely a matter of simple arithmetic. Apart from Barnaby James' equal determination, and skill that was little less than Johnny's, there was the matter of brakes. For hours after the crash they had remained as good as they had ever been, but under the terrific strain of twenty-three hours' hard cornering they were now beginning to show signs of unevenness and wear. The soaked track had added new demands on them, and now Johnny found himself having to apply them earlier at the corners and to make greater use of his gear-box.

Then there were *Diane*'s tyres. He had known they were going to be an anxiety, and the next forty-five minutes were going to be crucial. He knew that there was almost no tread left. And if the front tyres were so worn, then the rear tyres, with the much greater wear they had to take, would be down almost to the canvas. Cornering in the wet flat-out at Le Mans on smooth tyres was no joke.

But it was no use worrying. That gap had to be closed, the Atlantic had to be caught and passed. It was a time for nerveless determination and complete concentration. . . .

The flying cloud of spray, with the dark dot of the racing machine in the centre of it, was no nearer the next time round, Johnny reckoned. And Mervyn's signal confirmed it – '25' hung out from the Bentley pit. The gap was widening again. Johnny shrugged his shoulders. All right, all right then. . . .

Like any Olympic runner, like any professional athlete, Johnny knew from years of experience of motor-racing that there was always a reserve of strength to draw on. He knew that, even after he had reached the point when he was sure he could drive no faster, when he was taking every corner at the absolute limit, there was a fraction more speed to be drawn from the car, one more degree of courage to be exploited.

Before the dangerous Esses he began leaving his foot on the accelerator just that fraction of a second longer. He discovered a few inches more road on the right of the track, over the thick white line and on to the rough sandy surface of the verge, before going into the corner, and a few inches more road on the left coming out. It was a desperate expedient, but it saved him nearly half a second.

At Tertre Rouge there had been oil on the track for hours from a car with a broken sump. Everyone had crept around gingerly, treating it as if the road surface were made of ice. Johnny was the first to discover that the incessant rain and frequent applications of sand had reduced the danger. On one lap he experimented cautiously, forcing *Diane* into a deliberate skid. On the next lap he went through ten miles an hour faster than Barnaby James.

Once again he passed Mike, giving himself a lap's lead over the third car. It was twenty to four when Johnny whipped the Bentley out of Arnage and, breaking out of the pinewoods, caught a brief glimpse of the Atlantic going through White House. Number '8' hung out in Mervyn's hands as he roared between the stands; and the Atlantic pit was a packed mass of white, anxious faces.

Johnny knew that Barnaby James was fighting as he had never fought before. Johnny had driven against him often, but he had never seen him drive like this. For three complete laps Johnny clung grimly to his tail, half-blinded by spray and dancing in his slipstream when the track of the cars crossed one another on the corners. A dozen times Johnny drew out to pass, closing in on those last few yards, but unable to complete the movement. Close to the end of Mulsanne he had drawn level with the Atlantic, and the two cars had screamed along side by side, for more than a mile, their engines strained to the limit. Johnny was actually a wheel length ahead at the warning sign for the corner, but the Atlantic, being on the inside, had got around a yard in front and the Bentley fell back again.

The hands of the big clock showed five minutes to four. In the A.C.O's office the chequered flag was being lifted down from its special shelf, and the president, heavy raincoat buttoned to his neck, was preparing to walk out on to the track.

Up in the press stand a hundred reporters and motoring correspondents were completing their dispatches in a dozen languages, their typewriters tapping out the final phrases honouring the gallant effort of the old Bentley. '. . . incredible feat to stay the course and to challenge to the last the fastest cars built today. . . .' '. . . But modern technical advances,' ran another report, 'must tell in the end, and in spite of . . .' For the last time they had come around the Atlantic had been ahead by more than fifty yards. It had been a breathtaking battle to the end, and there was no doubt that the sympathy of the packed thousands of spectators was with the veteran Speed Six.

But in motor-racing there is no sentimentality. It was the fastest car that won; and, in spite of everything, the Atlantic was proving herself just that little bit faster.

The crowds at Tertre Rouge saw Johnny brake and change down faultlessly. If the battered Bentley, with her crumpled mudguard and headlamp, her scratched and torn bodywork, bore the scars of the contest, her engine beat was as regular and sound as on the first lap twenty-four hours earlier. But in the driver's seat Johnny sat up as straight as a totem pole, relaxed and at ease with his arms extended to the wet steering-wheel and his visor streaming with water.

For everyone else Le Mans was over, the issue decided: Atlantic, Bentley, Atlantic in the first three places. Only for Johnny – and for the five in the Bentley pit who, taut with anxiety, knew his supreme ability – was this year's Le Mans an open race.

'The fastest car wins' – the most overworked and truest axiom in racing. But a car is something more than a complex and ingenious assembly of machinery. Those who work and live with fast cars believe they have a soul and a will to win; and the older and more loved a car, the more responsive and the more determined she can be.

For fear of being laughed at, Johnny Wild has not to this day divulged to anyone his certainty that it was the sudden memory of the great days of her *marque*, the years of victory at Le Mans some twenty-five years before, the inspiration of Woolf Barnato and Commander Glen Kidston's Speed Six which had roared past the chequered flag in 1930, that gave *Diane* the extra ounce of power to bring her alongside the Atlantic on Mulsanne again.

If he was to get by on this last lap, Mulsanne seemed to provide the only possible opportunity. He was almost a length ahead near the corner; another yard or two and he could slip in front and over to the right at the apex of the corner.

Johnny kept his foot on the accelerator until long past the danger point. The white barriers, the garish advertisement banners rushed towards him at a terrific speed. He saw the cloaked gendarmes, the marshals scattering away in alarm. Then he threw all his weight on the brake pedal and jerked the gear-lever straight into second.

Johnny never knew how he got around Mulsanne corner on that last lap. *Diane*'s great weight sent her massive body slewing from side to side; but her superb suspension kept her four wheels on the road, and she somehow drifted around under control, although sand from the bank sprayed up and flew in a blinding cloud at the spectators.

The two cars had gone through the corner side by side, and they came out dead level. Foot by foot now Johnny crept ahead – half a length – a length – by the next right-hander nearly two lengths, and he could swing over to the right and take the corner on the inside.

Through the pinewoods they roared, *Diane*'s deep, masculine exhaust note booming out and echoing among the trees like a triumphant trumpet-call. He was two lengths ahead at Arnage . . . then catastrophe.

For five laps, without Johnny being aware of it, the white strip of canvas – a warning sign on any car, a signal of deadly danger on a racing-car – had been growing wider on *Diane*'s rear wheels. It was a miracle they had lasted so long at the heat Johnny was generating in them by his furious driving. At Arnage, the last sharp corner on the last lap of the race, the final resistance of the left rear tyre cracked.

Johnny was dragging the Bentley out of the fierce drift with a delicate dab on the accelerator when he heard a violent explosion, and the rear of the car dropped. At the same moment the steering-wheel was dragged out of his hands and the car went into a frantic broadside slide down the centre of the road.

Behind him he heard the rending sound of tearing metal as the torn fragments of the cover ripped through the light steel of the mudguard and momentarily locked the wheel solid. The Bentley slewed like a stricken bison; but Johnny never allowed her to come to a standstill. Even while the crisis was at its height, he knew that above everything else he must keep *Diane* moving, that in spite of the blow-out he had a race to win. Nothing must be allowed to snatch victory away from him after the supreme effort he and his car had made to get ahead.

Luckily for them both, Barnaby James' reactions were razor-sharp. He had been doing fifty through Arnage, but at the instant that he saw Johnny skate across the road he jammed on his brakes, and the Atlantic came to a shuddering halt amid a blue cloud of burning rubber. His engine stalled, and Johnny was away again, beating up the track on three tyres and a bare metal wheel rim with a sound like a steam-roller going through a scrapyard.

It was more than two miles to the finishing line; Johnny had a lead of a quarter of that distance. With a crippled car it did not seem possible that he could hold off the Atlantic.

The agonized crowds, craning over each other's heads and pushing forward in their excitement, watched the distance between the two cars close. It was four hundred yards at White House, three hundred at the beginning of the rise up to the grandstands, then two hundred, a hundred yards. The great roar from the massed spectators drowned the noise of the straining cars – even the metallic clatter of the wheel rim biting into the asphalt.

The rain had ceased suddenly on that last lap, and Johnny saw the white blocks of the concrete stands as a flickering, dazzling blur in a shaft of sunlight, as beguiling and welcoming as the mosques of a desert city to a weary traveller. He was hardly aware that this was a race, the finish of Le Mans. Dazed and at the last stages of exhaustion, he knew only that he was driving at a great speed, that it was still not fast enough, and that he must get to the top of the rise ahead. It was all that mattered.

And he could do no more. There were no more corners to drift around, to time to a split second. His foot was locked hard on the accelerator.

He was not aware of the little green car just behind, he did not see it creeping up on his left, yard by yard, foot by foot. He never saw it draw level alongside, forge ahead at first slowly and then more rapidly. . . . Johnny Wild was past all knowledge.

He was the only one among the thousands who failed to see the chequered flag sweep down in his honour when he crossed the line half a length ahead of the Atlantic and just before it got ahead of him.

And then some blessed instinct of self-preservation caused his right foot to switch from accelerator to brake pedal.

Diane swayed and rocked to a standstill just beyond the pit area, her driver slumped over the steering-wheel.

'Clean him up a bit for the cameras,' shouted Blackie above the uproar. 'Can't have our Johnny all stained and oily in the papers.'

But the cameramen were not going to wait while Mervyn washed Johnny down and combed his hair.

This was how a hero should look – grimy, drawn and exhausted. There was even the suggestion of a hero's grin-after-the-ordeal playing about Johnny's mouth as he was held up on the back of the driver's seat by Mervyn on one side and Blackie on the other. A damp towel had brought him around quickly enough; a quick drink and he was ready to be dragged out of the seat and into the glare of world publicity.

No doubt the ambulance men would have liked to have got hold of him again. But the President of France himself could not have found a passage through the storming, milling mob of officials and marshals, pressmen and photographers, mechanics, drivers – and now the spectators, who were swarming over the barriers sweeping aside the line of helpless gendarmes.

From somewhere or other there appeared the wreaths of victory, garlands of flowers that were draped around Johnny's shoulders, an opened bottle of champagne and a glass to drink it from.

A battling figure with a microphone forced his way up to the car and thrust the instrument before Johnny's face. '*Un mot, un mot s'il vous plaît, monsieur,*' he begged.

And Johnny's tentative grin broadened. Victory had its obligations, that he knew. He took the microphone in his hand, and spoke the first words since he had set off from the pits more than two hours before.

'There's not much to say,' he said hoarsely. 'Haven' had much time to gather my thoughts yet. But that last lap was a bit of a do. Yes,' he said decidedly, 'quite a do. What the newspapers like to call a "close-fought contest with the excitement sustained to the last moment."'

Johnny took a sip of champagne and looked thoughtful. He was obviously expected to say something generous about his opponent. But he would have choked over the words. So he compromised, and said into the microphone, 'I'm grateful to Number 8 Atlantic for one thing at least and that is for giving me my hardest-won victory since I began motor-racing. Thank you – in spite of everything, Mr James – thank you for that. . . .'

The cheers were renewed, and when they had died away, Johnny spoke again, this time solemnly and sincerely. 'This Bentley victory, the first for so long, could not have happened without the work of three people. First, W. O. Bentley himself, who designed *Diane*, and is one of the greatest engineers of the century. Second, the chief engineer Mervyn Williams, who tuned and prepared the car. And third, my co-driver, who played such a magnificent part in the struggle.'

Johnny drew his two friends up beside him on the back of the front seat, and the crowd turned the car and began to push it back towards the pits. With his speech completed, Johnny looked about on all sides, and at last spotted among the seething mass of humanity the prominent deer-stalker hat of the Duke of Bucks. He waved him over, and the Duke was hoisted aboard, too.

'Sit down in the back, sir,' Johnny bawled. 'You're part of this team. And I'd have added my thanks over the radio if they hadn't snatched it away.'

The Duke knew his quiet voice would be lost in this storm of shouting, so he just smiled proudly and waved a hand at the three of them, while *his* Bentley was pushed forward along the track under the impetus of a hundred hand-power.

Chapter 10

A Golden Occasion

THE sky above the French countryside was bright blue. The road ahead was straight and wide and smooth. *Diane*'s engine was beating out a steady, powerful rhythm. And Johnny Wild's heart was full of joy and song.

'Throw out the Stuttkas, the B.R.C's,' he sang in a loud, unmusical voice:

> 'The Pegosos you can melt down for scrap,
> Chuck to the junk man the Rampinis,
> They're lousy and ghastly, a dreadful death-trap.
> As for the Atlantic,
> If you're not sick
> Of that frightful phoney car,
> The best we feel for that automobile,
> Is to take it to pieces and then,
> Tell Barnaby James, firmly but gently . . .'

He turned to Mervyn at his side. 'Not bad, eh?' he said.

Mervyn, who had suffered from Johnny's rhyme-making many times before, grimaced and sighed. 'Might be better if you started again and gave your whole mind to it.'

'Meaning, of course, that you would like to take over the wheel,' said Johnny, who had been resisting Mervyn's attempts to get into *Diane*'s driver's seat ever since they had left Le Mans.

'Have a heart,' begged Mervyn. 'We shan't have the old dear much longer.'

'Come now,' said Johnny, who was determined that nothing was going to spoil the delight of his last drive. 'You've forgiven me for that now. We've another £1,000 from the Duke, £1,500 prize money, bonuses to come from the oil and petrol companies, and enough publicity for "Eds and Vins" to set us back on our feet.'

He clapped Mervyn on the back. 'Don't be depressed, my old Welshman. Obviously a true driver's blood flows in your veins, and the moment we get back I'll teach you to drive every car we've got in stock. But,' he added cautiously, 'perhaps we'll have our lessons on the air-field.'

For the sheer joy of it, he pressed his foot down on the accelerator and *Diane* leaped ahead.

'Throw out the Stuttkas . . .' he began to sing again, moving his head from side to side in time with his song. The raucous, tuneless noise blended with the bellow of the Speed Six's exhaust, causing quiet-living, industrious French farm-workers to raise their heads from their toil in the fields.

'Dieppe 45 km,' said the milestone. They would soon be there now. 'Be glad to see the old white cliffs again, eh, Mervyn?' said Johnny. 'Though we'll have a couple of hours to put away until Blackie and the truck turn up.'

They breasted a rise with 120 m.p.h. on the speedometer. The road ran straight ahead, dead straight for mile after mile. 'Wonderful motoring, wonderful car,' thought Johnny in delight. The only other car in sight was three miles ahead, and they were overtaking it rapidly. As they approached it and it began to take on a shape, Johnny looked at it with more interest. Those contours seemed somehow familiar. Then, while he was still puzzling, the car drew in at the roadside and he saw a small, black figure climb out. At the same moment he called to Mervyn excitedly, 'D'you know what that is ahead? That, my dear old ace driver, is an Atlantic.'

It was an Atlantic, and it was in trouble. Johnny slowed at once and brought *Diane* to a standstill just ahead of the sports car. With mixed delight and amazement he saw the number '8' on the tail, and recognized the smooth, dapper figure of Barnaby James leaning over the open bonnet. 'This is going to be some reunion,' he muttered to Mervyn before climbing out.

But, like most easily-forgiving people with a generous character, Johnny felt strangely embarrassed when he came face to face with his old opponent. Stumbling over his words, he asked Barnaby James what the trouble was; and the Atlantic driver, visibly terrified by the sudden appearance of the man he had been prepared to murder the day before, kept as far away from Johnny as he could. 'Spot of ignition trouble, I reckon,' he mumbled, and buried his face in the engine again.

The Atlantic service trucks and trailers had left the evening before. Johnny had seen them depart. Barnaby James had perhaps had business to conduct in Paris – and with dismissal awaiting him when he got back to Atlantic Motors he would be looking for a new job – and had chosen to drive back on his own. In any case, the unwritten rule of the road demanded that they should halt and give what assistance they could.

Mervyn's intentions as he followed Johnny towards the Atlantic were, however, more dramatic. In fact, he decided, there was a nice touch of diabolism about his plan.

After a quick glance at the Atlantic's engine, Mervyn ordered Barnaby James into the driver's seat, and told him to switch on the ignition. 'I'll soon fix this for you,

Mr James,' he said brightly, and he gave Johnny a screwdriver and told him to hold it on the distributor contact points and watch them carefully.

'I'll just get my tool-roll,' Mervyn said, and scurried forward to *Diane*. It was under the driver's seat, and the tightly coiled length of rope, stowed beside it, was concealed hastily under his overcoat.

Mervyn hurried back to the Atlantic, and he flung himself on the ground under the car's front axle. 'I think it's this lead just here,' came his muffled voice from below. 'Switch on now, Mr James. And, Johnny, keep that screwdriver on the points.'

But Mervyn's activities had nothing to do with the Atlantic's electrical equipment. With deft fingers he drained the fluid from the brakes' hydraulic reservoir, knotted one end of the rope tightly around the front axle and, concealed by the front of the car, crawled the few feet to the Bentley's rear axle. A double slip-knot now linked the two machines, and Mervyn set about stage three of his hastily-contrived plan.

'Hang on one moment,' he called breathlessly. 'Need another spanner.' And he darted back to *Diane*'s driver's seat.

The Bentley's engine started at once. An experienced driver now, Mervyn slipped her into first, revved her up, and engaged the clutch smoothly.

All this happened in no more than three seconds, and Johnny had leaped back from the suddenly moving Atlantic and Mervyn had the two cars at running speed before he realized what was happening.

Mervyn heard no more than confused shouting from behind as he sped away. He had *Diane* up to sixty before he looked back over his shoulder; and the picture behind him brought an expression of puckish delight to his face.

The Atlantic's bonnet had slammed shut, and he had a perfect view of Barnaby James half-standing on the driver's seat, one hand on the steering-wheel, the other waving frantically in the air; his red hair – usually slicked smooth and flat over his head – flew wildly in the wind; and his mouth was wide open in silent, helpless protest.

Far back down the road Mervyn could just see the tiny figure of Johnny, standing with his hands on his hips while he watched the two cars disappear. 'Ah, he won't mind,' Mervyn reassured himself. 'He'll probably get as much fun as me out of this. And Blackie'll be along soon. ... Hey ho for Dieppe!' And he pressed the accelerator hard down, and the cars flew like the wind across the rolling French countryside. ...

The entry into the French town of Dieppe was all that Mervyn had hoped it would be. Every Frenchman – and the French view motor-racing as the English view cricket or the Americans baseball – had read of *Diane*'s startling victory at Le Mans. Heads turned in the crowded streets at the sound of her low, beating exhaust note, and shouts of recognition were followed by surprised cries when they saw she had the defeated Atlantic in tow.

Gusts of laughter arose from the pavements. Here was ultimate humiliation for the defeated Atlantic and splendid triumph for the old car that critics had wanted to remove from the Le Mans circuit because she might block the road.

Mervyn crawled along through the thick traffic, driving with complete assurance but with great care, for the only means Barnaby James had of slowing his car was the hand transmission brake which was weak and worn, and the Atlantic had already shunted into the back of the Bentley several times.

Word of their arrival flashed like wildfire through the town, and by the time tower and towed arrived at the docks quite a crowd had collected. The moment the two cars had halted on the dock, Barnaby James leaped out of his machine and, without a word, dived through the crowd and disappeared among the side-streets. The whole business had become too much for him.

Mervyn, however, enjoyed himself hugely. The Frenchmen swarmed around the car as if he had just crossed the finishing line; and, of course, no one doubted for a moment that this was Johnny Wild – the great Johnny Wild, hero of Le Mans' greatest battle. For a while Mervyn protested, but no one listened, so without too much reluctance he allowed himself to be fêted. . . . Autographs had to be signed and the heads of little boys patted. The bouquets of flowers piled up around him in *Diane*; the local newspaper reporter extracted a long account of the race in garbled French and hesitant English.

Blackie steered their little service truck along the narrow street leading to the docks. A short way ahead a solid mass of people blocked their way to the dock.

'Quite a crowd,' said Johnny. 'Funny place to have a fair. I wonder where old Mervyn's hidden *Diane* – if he ever got here.'

'I'm glad we spoke to that old crook,' said Johnny some four hours later after they had crossed the Channel. 'I shouldn't really have been happy leaving him like that.'

Blackie nodded his head in agreement. 'If ever there

was an example of pride taking a fall, Barnaby James was it,' he said. 'Poor old chap. Wonder what he'll do now?'

'Oh, come, don't let's get mawkish about him,' protested Johnny. 'He'll be all right. He's in the championship class as a driver, even if he does tear his cars to bits. Any of the big Continental teams'll have a place for him.' He slowed *Diane* for the big town ahead. Only thirty more miles to their garage. . . .

And yet there had been something pretty sad about the huddled figure in the corner of the Channel steamer's lounge, and it was Johnny who had suggested that there would be nothing to lose by inviting him over to their corner. The Bentley team could afford to be generous, and they were, though Barnaby James' sour defensiveness had been hard to break down.

There had been no mention of Jon Jeans' attempt to drive *Diane* off the road, beyond Blackie's inquiry after his condition, and their conversation had been stilted and embarrassed and brief. Barnaby James' resentment, it seemed to them, had thawed enough to reveal his surprise that they were having anything to do with him at all. Anyway, the gesture had been made, they had all shaken hands, and it was quite understood between them that, so long as he played a clean racing game in future, they would at least be on speaking terms.

Behind them Harry was driving the service truck; Mervyn, sleepy after the excitement of the morning, was dozing among the stacked equipment in the back.

'Another half-hour with *Diane*,' said Johnny sadly.

'Never mind, it was worth it – worth it a hundred times,' said Blackie. 'And the Duke'll let us take her out when we feel like a spin around, I expect. Shouldn't be surprised if he asks us to race her for him.'

'That'll be some consolation, but it'll never be quite the same again without the old girl.'

It was dusk when they sighted the low buildings of their garage on the edge of the old airfield. It would be good to be home, to get back to business. . . .

Johnny switched on the surviving headlight and slowed for the turning off the main road. There was Blackie's new signboard: 'Eds and Vins'. There were the padlocked gates. . . . But they were not padlocked, they were wide open. And there was a light on in Blackie's office. Johnny accelerated up their drive, ready to leap out. There was a man, running towards them, waving his arms.

'Hey,' yelled Blackie, 'what the – ' But his voice trailed away. Clearly picked out in the powerful beam was the lean, loose figure of Mike Corrigan, waving and smiling as he ran towards them.

He leaned over *Diane*'s windscreen, laughing and panting. 'I thought you might do me in as a burglar,' he said. 'Hope you don't mind the one-man committee of welcome.'

'Like it,' said Johnny. 'Like it a lot. But tell us the whys and the wherefores.'

'A brew of tea first,' answered Mike. 'I reckoned that's what you'd want after your tiring day. Come on in. It's all ready.'

Bewildered and intrigued, Johnny and Blackie followed Mike into the office, where a kettle was boiling on the gas-ring. Mervyn joined them, and then Mike told them his story.

It was brief and not long in the telling. Sickened by Barnaby James' methods, he had written out his resignation immediately after the race and left it in the Atlantic pit. 'I know he's got the sack by now, anyway,' said

Mike. 'But I wouldn't serve with that organization any more, anyway. They're a tough crowd of ruthless tycoons. I flew back last night and talked it all over with my wife. She's willing to take the risk, and I'm willing, too – though I know your leanest days are probably behind you now – if you'd like me to – to,' he stumbled over his words – 'well, to join up with you. It'll be good fun, and we can race together at the week-ends.'

A chorus of joy greeted this suggestion. 'Of course, Mike.' 'Best news yet.' 'The team'll be complete again now.' This was wonderful.

'Thanks, thanks a lot,' said Mike. 'I don't know what I'd have done if you'd said no. In fact,' he added, looking decidedly embarrassed, 'it would have been deuced awkward.'

'Why? What's up?'

'Well,' said Mike, laughing awkwardly. 'I've twice represented myself as a director of "Eds and Vins".'

'Once was at the police station,' Blackie prompted. 'They gave you the keys to the place, I expect.'

Mike nodded. 'And when I came along here at lunch time there was a chap wondering when you'd be open for business. So, feeling a bit mad after all the excitement, I told him we were open for business now.'

'Did he buy anything?' Blackie asked.

'Well, no. Actually . . .' and Mike buried his face momentarily in his tea mug. 'Actually I bought something from him. Said we'd pay him tomorrow.' He looked around at the three anxious faces. 'Hope I haven't started off on the wrong foot. I realize I don't know too much about Vintage cars, but she looked such a nice example –'

Anything further he had to say about the car he had bought was lost in the shout that suddenly echoed in the yard outside. 'Mr Wild, Mr Black,' came Harry's excited voice. 'Come here quickly. Look at this.'

They all ran for the door and dashed out into the night. The apprentices had turned *Diane* around and parked her in her position of honour. But by what Johnny took to be some trick of the light, her headlamp appeared to be focused on herself. It was all very odd. There seemed to be two Bentleys in the yard suddenly, and between them, waving his hands and beckoning them over, was Harry the apprentice.

'Look, sir, look what we've found,' he called.

Mervyn, Johnny, and Blackie stood on the steps staring unbelievingly at the two cars. Apart from the painted '1' on *Diane*'s bodywork there seemed to be no difference between them.

Mike's voice came from behind them. 'Oh, yes,' he said casually in his slow Irish drawl. 'That car. That's the one I've bought. Have I done something awful?'

'Awful?' said Johnny in a half-strangled, distant sort of voice. 'Unless we're all mad, you've done something impossible.'

'Pinch me, Johnny,' Blackie murmured. 'I'm dreaming. I know I'm dreaming.'

Even Mervyn's voice sounded far away and not quite his own. 'That, Mike my boy, is a 1930 team Le Mans Speed Six Bentley, the one that came in second behind *Diane*, in 1930. It's not possible, man, but that's what it is.'

And he was right, as a glance at the engine number and at the chassis quickly revealed.

'Hope I did right,' said Mike nervously when they returned to the office. He was still feeling rather bewildered by the excitement. 'And I hope I didn't pay too much for her. Was £100 too much, do you reckon, Blackie?'

*

Limborough Park was looking its loveliest in the June morning sunshine. The rhododendrons and azaleas were at their richest, the fresh new beech leaves sparkled in great rolling waves of green on their branches, and the deer, with their young fawns beside them, grazed on the grassy slopes rising to the old house above them.

The signs of welcome, however, did not add to the beauty of the park, though they were appreciated by the occupants of the two Speed Six Bentleys that drove carefully up the gravel drive. 'Welcome Back, Heroes' they read on the banners stretched between the trees. 'We Salute the Great Bentley Triumph.' 'Vintage Cars Forever.' 'Welcome, *Diane*, Queen of Them All.' They drove under one after another.

'That's really nice of the old Duke,' commented Johnny.

'And take a look at what we're coming to,' said Blackie, pointing ahead to the sweep of gravel drive at the front of the house. 'A real committee of welcome this time. That brass, Johnny! They must keep a special tank of the polish.'

Ranged symmetrically in a double semicircle before the front door was the whole of the Duke of Bucks' collection of Vintage and Edwardian cars – a breathtaking assembly of gleaming brass, silverwork, polished mahogany, and immaculate paint. In front of them all, like a general before his paraded troops, stood the magnificent Silver Ghost Rolls-Royce; and sitting at the wheel was the Duke himself. He had been expecting them at ten o'clock, and they had arrived on time.

Johnny changed gear delicately, and slowed *Diane* to walking pace. 'Oh, heavens, Blackie, I hope this is going to be all right.' They were not going to take the Duke's thousand pounds; that they had settled between them. The Speed Six was no longer unique, and they had replaced her for a paltry hundred pounds. What had worried them was the Duke's disappointment. To a fanatical collector there was all the difference in the world between the possession of a unique motor-car and one of which there was another example in existence – and the new Speed Six had been as beautifully maintained as *Diane*.

But they need not have worried, for they had underestimated the Duke's generous nature. When the two Bentleys drew up beside the Rolls, he stared at them in startled amazement for a moment. He was smiling merrily as he climbed out of the driver's seat and doffed his deer-stalker in greeting.

'Well, well,' he murmured. 'Goodness gracious me! So we were all under a misapprehension, were we? All my words of welcome and congratulation will have to be repeated. You have not only proved to the world that *Diane* is the greatest car, but you have produced a twin for her. Magnificent, magnificent,' he said reverently as he walked slowly round the new Bentley. 'Hardly credible if it were not here before my eyes, this is the machine, is it not, which Mr Clement and Mr Watney drove into second place at Le Mans in 1930?'

After being introduced to Mike and commending him on his good sense in conducting the deal on his own initiative, he took Johnny and Blackie by the arm and led the four of them on to the terrace where refreshments were laid out for them on a table.

'And now,' said the Duke shyly when they were all seated, 'if you'll forgive me, I've got a little surprise for you.' He drew from his pocket a small wooden box. 'I knew there were going to be two Speed Six Bentleys here this morning, though I certainly never expected a third.

I had this little trophy made up a week before Le Mans,' he continued, taking a quantity of tissue paper from inside the box. 'If you hadn't won, it might have been some consolation for a gallant try. But I had an idea you were going to bring her home first. And you did – so . . .'

The Duke revealed from the wrapping an exquisitely modelled replica of *Diane*, a masterpiece of craftsmanship in solid gold, exact in every minute detail of the Bentley's construction.

The Duke held it for a moment in his gnarled old hands then he looked at Johnny with a smile, beckoned him forward, and with a little bow, presented it to him.

'If you like,' he said merrily, relieved that the brief ceremony was over, 'you can say that it is in honour of a great-hearted car that for twenty-four hours stood up to the wildest Johnny Wild driving any car has suffered.' They all laughed with the Duke, and glanced down from the terrace to the scarred *Diane* on the drive.

'I wish you had let us tidy her up before delivering her,' said Blackie. 'We've never sold a car in that condition before.'

The Duke shook his head. 'It'll be an honour and a pleasure to repair the wounds of Le Mans,' he said. 'The trouble is, my cars don't get knocked around enough. There's nothing I enjoy more than working on them, but there's usually nothing for me to do except polish. They're nearly all better than the day they left their coachbuilders.'

Gratitude expressed for the magnificent gift, refreshment consumed, they returned to the cars. For half an hour they strolled among the Duke's priceless collection, then they piled into their new Bentley and waved goodbye.

'Bring *Diane* over to the garage and we'll try the two

old girls out against one another,' Johnny suggested to the Duke.

'That would be a sight worth seeing,' agreed the Duke. 'I'd give you a run for your money, Johnny, even if I'm a bit deaf and my eyes aren't what they used to be.'

Johnny started up, and the Bentley rolled forward.

'Good-bye.'

'Good-bye.'

'Good-bye, sir.'

'Thanks again – and be kind to our beautiful *Diane*.'

Slowly, and with hardly a sound, the big green car drifted down the drive between the old beech trees, across the deer park, was lost to sight among the rhododendrons. It was not until she had passed through the lodge gates that the Duke heard the sudden roar of her exhaust across the park. The sound rose and fell, rose and fell again as Johnny changed gear . . . and then it became fainter and fainter until the Duke was left in a silent world of his own in front of his house.

About the Author

Bruce Carter's real name is Richard Hough. He was born in 1922, and went to a co-educational school. He was a fighter bomber pilot in the R.A.F. during the war, and received some of his training in south Californian army camps.

He has written several children's books, and is part-time children's editor for Hamish Hamilton and for Transworld Publishers. His wife Charlotte is an artist and book illustrator, and does some writing too, and even his three daughters produce their own magazine *The Tudor Express*.

Richard Hough's main interests are early railways, motoring, and children's books. He writes of this book: 'For years the atmosphere of British and European racing circuits has had a fascination for me; this is most acute at the Le Mans twenty-four-hour race, and I cannot imagine that any author can remain unaffected by it. I have always loved vintage cars; I once owned a thirty-year-old Rolls-Royce which was like new and completely silent only rather heavy to handle in London's traffic.

'These two loves linked naturally together – and thus *Speed Six*.'

Some other Puffin books you might enjoy are described on the following pages.

The Twenty-Two Letters

Clive King

Long ago, 1500 years before Christ was born, when King Minos of Crete still worshipped the bull, when the Eastern Mediterranean was divided into many unstable little states, and Egyptian writing was a sacred and secret cult, Resh the master builder lived in the city of Byblos with his three sons and his daughter.

Resh was very busy building a new palace for the King, but his three sons went off in different directions. All the time they were away their father and sister Beth were waiting anxiously for their safe return with the presents they should give the King on his Day of Offering. But despite the unheard-of way Aleph sent a message warning the King of his enemies' approach, nothing could prevent the disaster which the strange man from the eastern land of Chaldea had foretold.

Jennings goes to School

Anthony Buckeridge

'Jennings, what does a bat do in winter?'
'It – er – it splits if you don't oil it, sir.'

Even if he isn't always as attentive as his master would wish, J. T. C. Jennings is a well-meaning, cheerful and obliging boy, and it seems surprising that his arrival at Linbury Court Preparatory School should cause life there to become so hectic, hilarious, and generally unpredictable.

His intentions are always good and there is no doubt that his serious-minded friend Darbishire ought to be a soothing influence, but between them they are responsible for a number of hair-raising incidents, including the false fire alarm and the Poisonous Spider.

Starman Jones
Robert A. Heinlein

This is a story of the world in 200 years' time, when rockets to the moon are as commonplace as trains to Ealing, and weekly space ships loaded with supplies and settlers leave for the planets are regularly as our ships now sail to Europe.

Max Jones is an orphan who dreams of being an astrogator. He insinuates himself aboard the 'Asgard', but there is a mistake in calculation and instead of making the planned leap of 97 light years they enter another galaxy and are obliged to land on an unknown star. This turns out to be inhabited by flying jellyfish and a strange kind of centaur who use men as beasts of burden. Max and Ellie, the girl he wants to marry, are captured and there are some hair-raising adventures and dramatic decisions to be made before Max is able to make the calculations which will take them back through the 'Hole' to their known planet.

For readers of 11 up who are interested in the world of the future.

The Cave
Richard Church

John Walters sat on a rock wishing the summer holidays had been more exciting and watching an unseen animal pushing like a submarine through the bracken. But why did the movement stop so suddenly? That was the start of the terrific adventure which finished the holidays in a blaze of excitement. For the animal had disappeared into an undiscovered cave, and John and his friends could not rest until they had explored the cave's mysteries.

But it is what happens to them *inside* the cave which makes this book especially exciting, for the characters of the five friends change and develop in face of the dangers they encounter.

Master of Morgana

Allan Campbell McLean

A story set in the Isle of Skye. Niall the sixteen year old hero, attempts to discover the reason for his brother's nearly fatal accident at the salmon fisheries, and finds himself caught up in ghost hunting, treasure hunting, smuggling and attempted murder.

Jim Davis

John Masefield

Jim Davis was only 12 when he first met Marah, the brave, fierce, and chivalrous smuggler, and 13 when dismayed by having helped Marah's gang capture a coastguard. He sets off to free him and is instead press-ganged by the smugglers and forced to take part in their illegal runs to France. Under Marah's watchful eye he learns the arts of seamanship as well as smuggling, and when after hair-raising adventures he escapes, sets off on the long tramp home, and is captured by gypsies, it is Marah who turns up to rescue him.